Praise

Leave to Remain is back-to-front suit, a cascading Escher staircase, a Jacob's Ladder toy. Field and Lang's hybrid essay/ meditations bridge the gaps they create: fascinating, tricksy, eloquent, wistful, cosmic, joyous! —Joanna Walsh

A comic *tour de force* from the far reaches of sense. Thalia Field and Abigail Lang have produced a beguiling document that reveals the hilarity and unparalleled strangeness that arises when you pull the pin from language. —Ben Marcus

Thalia Field is a singular talent & unique literary force, forty years ahead of literature. There is no one writing like her. There's no one I'd rather read in English at this time. In *Leave to Remain*, her interrogative collaboration with Abigail Lang, we are alive to the possibilities of language. We are humored in the work's mapping, and intellectually entangled in the trapeze of its ideas. This work is pure delight. Literary ketamine. —Anakana Schofield

If Ovid had been in the blurbing business, I think he would have said that nothing in recent years has reinvoked Janus' importance or ridiculousness quite like Thalia Field and Abigail Lang's two-minded riff on what it means to be always and ever-present, and precisely nowhere in particular. —John D'Agata

Thalia Field and Abigail Lang

Leave to Remain
—— Legends of Janus

DALKEY ARCHIVE PRESS

Library of Congress Cataloging-in-Publication Data

Names: Field, Thalia, 1966- author. | Lang, Abigail, author.
Title: Leave to remain : legends of Janus / Thalia Field and Abigail
Lang.
Description: First edition. | McLean, IL : Dalkey Archive Press, 2020.
Identifiers: LCCN 2019043629 | ISBN 9781628972849 (trade
paperback ; acid-free paper)
Classification: LCC PS3556.I398 L43 2020 | DDC 813/.54--dc23
LC record available at https://lccn.loc.gov/2019043629

Dalkey Archive Press
McLean, IL / Dublin

Cover design by Dominique Pasqualini
Interior by Kirby Gann
Printed on permanent/durable acid-free paper.

www.dalkeyarchive.com

CONTENTS

But what divinity shall I describe you to be, double-shaped Janus? For Greece has no god like you. Tell, at the same time, the reason, why you alone, of the dwellers in the sky, see both what is at your back and what is before. While I was revolving thus in my mind, with tablet in hand, the house seemed brighter than before it was: then holy Janus, wondrous with his two-headed form, suddenly presented to my sight his double features. I was confounded, and felt my hair to stand on end with awe, and my breast was frozen with a sudden chill. Holding in his right hand a staff, and a key in his left, he uttered these sounds to me, from his front mouth.

Laying aside your apprehensions, poet who record the days, learn what you ask, and catch with all your mind my words. Me the ancients, for I am an old thing, called Chaos. See you of how remote a period I sing the occurrences.

Ovid, *Fasti*

Leave to Remain

Janus at a Chinese Restaurant in Paris

Did a doorway allow us to **hold up** despite desire?
Or were we already in the gap?

Consider Janus: two faces, one brain. Of a mind? Think twice.

How does it at the gate?

Which way does your beard point tonight?
Do omens attend upon beginnings?

Later may we break the cookie in two and split our fortune? Later
will the waiter come to take our order and, disobeying it, reveal
a scene playing on many fronts?

If luck is the past, will fortune show the future? Or is it the other
way, and the next thing will only return us to the past thing?
Later may we deadlock.

But that's ahead of ourselves.

First we must decide what kind of translation to pursue.
We've come here for a traditional meal in an unfamiliar
place. Or have we never met before now?
Did someone say we did?

*Two trains going in opposite directions leave the station at the same
time . . .*

(On the witness stand:) "Doorkeeper of the heavenly court /
I look towards both east and west at once."

Will I speak in your turn, and you speak in mine?

(On the witness stand:) "The ancients called me Chaos,
and even now, a sign of my once confused state, my front
and back appear the same."

We want to, we really try to, but looking as we do, we can
never look away. Yet do we see eye to eye?

Trusting the translator has never been easy; they know the
enemy language, we take their word for everything.

Show who you really are!

Easy for you to say. The waiters wait on our dropped
hints, gestures of readiness, menus in hand, names not
requested, eyes not met, stares not stared ("follow me" as
to a reader, not a hungry customer, or both?)

And our bumper sticker: "Don't fuck with me I have eyes
in the rear."

Generations **sanction** movement.
Time begins to end at a standstill.

First, Charlemagne couldn't tell dead pagans from his
own dead men, so he asked for a sign split in two: thorns
and briars grew up around the bodies of the pagans.

(Janus on the witness stand:) "My unbarred gate stands
open wide, so that when the people go to war the return
path's open too."

But why hide in peace, and open your gates in war?

Bar it in peacetime so peace cannot depart:
How can we understand the cult of "look-
both-ways-before-leaping"? Can we know the
instant the men became "bearded men"?

(A translation provides the first fiction, a double-invented
character, a metamorphosis.)

Hoist the flag, call men to arms.
Or recruit the vulnerable when they're wanting.
Trick or trap them into *vote* or *veto*, just a slip of a sound
between tongue and brain.

I think you're making a face at me, but I can never tell.

Disfigured, we are shown to a booth

(arranged for our particular handicap)
faces out, translated for our different tongues,
meaning is not at face value.

When the Romans wanted to declare formal war on Pyrrhus,
they captured an enemy soldier and sold him a lot of
Roman ground on which the *pater patratus* cast his javelin.

Hard **pits strike** us. Deep **pits strike** us out.

We flip the famous two-faced two faced coin.

Chinese restaurant, Paris between wars.
Can we agree to disagree? Let's admit the opposite, it will be
yesterday soon enough, and time is always extinction's game
plan, since we can't send it back.

Janus Quirinis ("god of the community of *Quirites* (citizens)")
vs. Mars ("god of the mass of *milites*")—their temples symmet-
rically bound—in other words, the need for fighting ourselves
was already set into stone across the *pomerium*—
If I nod down, you nod up, and I nod up, you nod down.
We try to agree: an international crime will be told.
Intelligence is simply privileged information.
What is the role of intelligence countering itself?
Are we just walk-ins making an entreaty?

Could our very form be treason? treachery? ambiguity?
Decisions must be made. Words are not currency, there is no
perfect translation, and someone always has a beard.

Reader, wherewith the faith? The hungry asses?
Wherefore mutant snakes and babies?
Whereof the two-faced cat?

In this establishment, the meal is expected to be edible
and remembered as inedible (or vice versa).

Double agents fill two mouths at once, **carrying on**.
(The gate, in Janus-speak, in new technologies,
passes the information through.)
Intelligence is mostly unverifiable because it is not public.
To be good, intelligence must lead to a decision.

For years I've been trying to get you to cross the line,
and you've been recruiting me back.
How have we remained such good friends
while staying on opposite sides?
Where would we break if we are told to break it off?

"You don't know me," says our T-shirt, in a foreign script.

"My name is X, I'll be your waiter."

Etruscans adopted a grid plan so spirits would cross the
city and leave more swiftly. The N–S axis (*cardo*) was ben-
eficial, but the E–W axis (*decumanus*) unfavorable—Here,
Janus guarded the northern entrance: one face turned
east, the other watching the west.

*plot: sun rises in the east / **puts out** clouds / sets in the west*

Aligned, the triumphant marched along the *via sacra*, the General waiting for the Senate to relieve him from the *imperium* (right to kill) before they filed through an archway like a stream, spanned—

Could the menu be more self-negating?

We **peruse** it.

Identical, twinned, hyphenated, banished, welcomed—
Are we such oxymorons, alone together?

We have intelligence on identities. One may be a rat. One may be some sort of White Devil. Liberties spread and die off like diseases. Insects become us. Fortune cookies follow, hidden in enemy camps, there is always a convenient shape and color.

But reader, the truth is we share internal organs in any language. We adopt phonetics to distinguish us, but really it's one gut feeling. Gates overlooking possibilities show the view we are born to. We could've learned anything from our blank beginnings / the portrait above us displays only a model of a portrait: a thing not quite itself standing for itself.

God of draughts, get the lazy Suzy to spin!

That we might share one empty stomach.
That we might not mention it.

Little dumpling, don't be happy/sad.

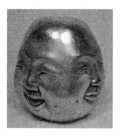

Janus, make these children into soldiers on their way out,
and change them back into good citizens when they return.

But how to **screen** the inner linings of the soul antagonist?
How to be sure the bilingual bride has no veiled intention?
Is a captured slave faithful to his listener?

How can we animate what is already **spirit**,
a living dead? Seeking **leave to remain**, can we
refrain at the peak of the march?

A good soldier pauses, waiting.

Heads or tails?

Flip a coin minted to commemorate the closing
of the gates of war. Not to **buckle** easily,
but to **garnish** the prize.

Janus, twinned outward from his brain, it was said, the very
temples cracked. A traitor comfortably straddles gaps.

How can we choose which bale to eat?
How can we choose to eat or drink?
(Buridan's Ass starves in our midst,
due to the gap in the waiter's attention.)

X reappears and marvels at the word choice.
He mentions a rabbit. But we don't eat our rabbits.
(his look: What do you do with them?)
One of us has translated badly.
Culturally we have different tastes.

You might say one defendant, **spliced** at the seam,
knew more about Santa Claus and yet—real and
not-real—he's **moot**, a *model* of a man gifting,
a model of a bearded man on a flying chair.

(And if you're into beards, let's recall Charlemagne, the
beard to end all beards: white as April flowers or driven
snows that freeze—stroked, tugged, rent, torn, clasped,
shaken out and sworn by throughout *The Song of Roland*.)

The waiter makes strangely artificial perambulations around the
booth to take our conflicting orders—
(Does confession come easiest from liars?)

It's the model's model we imagine, we repeat.

We'll have two of those to eat, but for real.
I'm both looking forward to it.

Two-faced, are we of one mind?
The answer could be tactical or strategic.

And nothing like a traitor to **lace** the plot, **adumbrate**
sides, create reversal, dialectic, suspense. Heroes make the
best double-crossers. Prefer one of noble stock, peer to
the betrayed party.
                  Reader: at the beginning, Janus **put out** armies.
          (Recall the fingers of our statue curled in odd positions.)

Loyalty oaths may be good for business, but beg to be broken.
National interest forces a misdirection of belonging:
"I will spend my money only where the Blue Eagle flies"—
yet treasonous fingers point to all exits.

The waiter brings a steamed flatfish with scallions—right-eyed,
protruding, lying blind. Could it be we too have been the site
of an ocular migration? To adapt to which dramatic conditions
have we evolved our soul of extreme asymmetry (and lacking
teeth on one side of the jaw) . . .
    and an extra order of hard-boiled eggs we ask to split with a
    hair.

The traitor **dusts** us lightly as he takes the order.
Does he add or remove a layer?
Ah, the Janus-words we live by, chatting about
seemingly random figures and flights of history . . .

Ganelon, arch-traitor of Christendom second only
to Iscariot? Wasn't he Roland's own stepfather and
Charlemagne's brother-in-law?
Didn't he betray Charlemagne's army to the Muslims,
leading to the massacre of the
rear guard? Wasn't he caught, shaved on both cheeks, and
torn limb from limb by four fiery horses?
Guilty and not-guilty: a whole
room of **peers puzzles** it out.

*Pulling out from the station carrying French Jews, one train takes
remaining Jews, some leave remaining French the other way—*

O history, are you for real? Or just a fickle model? Feckless?
Fungible? Are we of two minds?
Or only two faces and as many tongues?

A rich line of traitors, the *false geste,* threads from Judas,
Ganelon, issuing by prequel back to Doon (*ur-traitor,
late root in a tree growing from the top down—**putting
out** innumerable branches).

Traitors split their minds, no U-turn. Bad translators are
traitors (cf. "If you can't help betraying books, go shit
without a candle!").

Loyalty oaths seek to **stay** change, at least from the outside in, like a bridge that lifts and turns and falls both
ways: jinx!

"My friends, there is no friend."

We jinx each other with the same word,
the same expression faced differently.

Old crusades humor: "What
distinguishes a spy from a pilgrim?"

The bridge and the threshold and the man accused;
each headed one way and the other.

It hurts but not where you'd expect.

Right down the middle in fact is an area of an almost
pleasurable sensation, the likes of which can only be compared to sleeping on board a ship, or hanging
backward off a swing, tempered by a gravity
that grabs but can't **root** the body.

We eat. (We literally don't eat.)

At the seam we are guilty and not-guilty, accused
and yet still innocent of all that is put before us,
deceptively **sanctioned** to stand trial.

For a door may be told? A bridge may be double-crossed?

Where a gap is without passage, a bridge feels abundance.

Kafka: "*Brücke dreht sich um!*"

Two trains meet at the train station of Montoire-sur-le-Loir,
where Hitler and Pétain shake hands, the Maréchal introduc-
ing an "honorable collaboration" and great perplexity.

Puzzle before we speak, then double-speak.

The lines go two ways, jinxing knowledge.
They double back, harkening an echo.

*Two trains leave the station at the same
moment, traveling in opposite directions . . .*

"I should mention without going any further, any further on,
that I say *aporia* without knowing what it means."

Both Gane and Pétain wanted to **put out** war.
Ganelon betrays **sanguine** Roland, whose hero status
depends on perpetual war, still based on fidelity.

War have you waged, so on to war proceed,
what time from war will we draw back instead?
Tooting one's own horn makes a coward.

Roland strikes vigorously, cleaves helmet, nose, mouth,
teeth, the body through the coat, cuts the saddle and
deep into the horse's back.

The Emperor clasps his chin, his fingers tug his beard.

Faldrun of Pui through the middle slices: and the count
slices his right hand clean off. Then takes the head of
Jursaleu the Blond, and through the spine he slices that
pagan's horse—

> Maybe we're only a Janus section of a failed primeval
> man, and somewhere a headless body roams the earth in
> search of its former half—longing for the time we could
> roll over like tumblers with our legs in the air; this was
> when we wanted to run away together.

"When will time come that he from war draws back?"
"Never," says Guene,
"so long as lives Rollanz."

> Let's ask for the **bill**. Let's consider a scapegoat to boot
> because maybe we owe or maybe we're due.
> We each have different currency.
> Who is the infidel? What currency is loyalty?
> How faithful is the translation?
> We don't understand the value of the price.
> How can we settle this?

The trial must take place to judge where
the defendant will go . . . A **legendary** man accused of a
double-dealing, of giving the enemy secret intelligence.

Legendary Knights meet in the gap, valley heroes in their
faces **fighting with** each other in battle as traitors to one,
as shadows box, or proxies die, depending on the cross-
road, as Knights will **resign** their service, mirror-images
of each other, tit for tat, spies come in and spies remove.

He strikes Pinabel on the helmet down to the nostril and
leaves him cleft, brains oozing. All of his head was down
the middle shorn.

Ride through Warwick, ride through Warwick, but oh!
It's not England's. Those yanks took Coventry too!
Names spread onto new lands as though
they were blank, and waiting.

*Two stories leave the station at the same
time going in opposite directions . . .*

Meanwhile, Reader, we **enjoin** you: **stay fast**.

Intelligence will reveal its opposite.

One of us may be right back, **overlooking** the view.
Writing back, we either forget or we surveil.
That's the trade-craft. Where lights and stars **are out**
and must be **fixed**. Push-me, pull-you.
In parallel we **wind up** to **trim** the tale.

Santa-Janus.
Janus-Claus.

A partition maintains a raw and reopening seam, and this
for some reason is where tension wants to mount (at the
coupling, which joining, also indicates factions).
Weapons grow internal to a body, shared or unshared,
so we each perceive a different audience of
those who might also lack perspective.

It's hard for anyone else to tell exactly where the split
occurs because we ourselves can shift its tether.
Without a wall or fence or steel plate, the movements of
cells perpetrate endless incursions. It tickles as they pass.

Weathered, we **bolt** the meal
(it's a **contemporary handicap**.)

We **lease** the table with legacy on both realms of the coin.

We **cleave** our loyalty.
It's all **downhill** from here.

Whatever the pretext, we **adumbrate** what happens next.
When it's time to go, where will we head?

Never alone but always solitary, sitting at a
draughtsboard playing both sides**, copemates
bound** to win nothing at once.

Two stories depart in opposite directions,
from the station marked **X**.

Friends might remind us that this sentence is still not true.
As nothing can be true or false in war we are wont to
ravel the threads—
About his brain the very temples cracked.
His palate is cleft but he meows through both.

Two trains meet for dinner in Paris.
Whatever sentence my friend says is true.
City of double agents tattooed in invisible ink.
Somehow we will both miss what happens.
Boustrophedon,
—read to terrible

"Half of my host I leave you presently."

In this Chinese restaurant we are foreign and near home.
We call each other **villain** as only friends can.

Does one of us have red hair?
Does that cover a source of suspicion?
Is bias an imaginary other cheek?

Allies or enemies at the front line? We may go separately
on this. Reader, it is up to you to read the report.
It is up to the handler to read the source.

The traitor brings small change to the table.
The change we bring is a traitor's currency, an
interpreter's wager.

*Two trains meeting at a crossing must both stop at the same time
and neither shall start up again until the other has gone.*

Pit of diamond, pit of coal, the hands bleed, eyes may cry;
Janus, warlike (peacelike), stares into the memory of the
gate of the future.

Game over, change sides.

> Reader, this could truly be but a falsehood.
> This could be a model of something else.
> Reader, the value of intelligence is up to how you use it.

"A **Bridge** to Turn Around!"

It was on a bridge that our plan took shape, or maybe "shape" is too strong a word for a web without anchor points, for a plan that floats both forward and backward in space-time. The plan involves a mysterious character, B, and the possible **betrayal** of B's son, on a bridge infested with agents and translators.

> Yes, a bridge has a shape.
> It stands *and/or* or *both/and* and supports multiple crossings.
> It spans something that moves in the middle.
> On it, we face two winds without commitment.
> The double agent and the translator have a task:
> to cross one bounded territory into another
> without betraying the boundary.

> A bridge crossing a cold stream consists of a polished **word**. The word has an arch. An arch spans a sentence and bridges. No one need fear falling because of its breaking or bending, though ownership (fate) is always complicated.

Not that there's ever war without a decisive battle on a bridge, a last stand or an opening move. Castles and towers and fortresses lodge on bridge-backs to claim parasitical status, and the vast and binocular advantage of a view.

Sun Tzu said: "*Thus what enables the wise sovereign and the good general to strike and conquer and achieve things beyond the reach of ordinary men, is* **foreknowledge**. *Now this foreknowledge cannot be elicited from spirits; it cannot be*

*obtained inductively from experience, nor by any deductive
calculation. Knowledge of the enemy's dispositions can only be
obtained from other men."*

> This sort of knowledge is intelligence. It comes in
> disguise. It serves many masters meeting on a
> bridge to make themselves unknown.

> To call out a Judas: consider if that name praises
> or shames. An elect member of an inner circle, a
> Judas is looked upon but not seen, and only later
> they say, "Yes, I swear he did have two faces!"
> "Oh, how he knew to find the right cheek!"
> Fools, the senses.

At the castle window near the bridge sits B, very scrupulous
and precise about matters of honor and what's right, and care-
ful to observe and practice loyalty above all else. Beside him
stands his son, who always practices precisely the opposite—
for he finds his pleasure in disloyalty, and never wearies of vil-
lainy, treason, and felony. From their advantage they watch the
bridge and a double figure attempting to cross in trouble and in
pain, yet who later claims to have been vigorous and spritely.

B's intelligence is only as good as both footings of the bridge
his son builds. The future stands on capturing this information
quickly, decoding it properly.

B speaks in indecipherable sighs.

A bridge carries two names: on one side a nationalist, proud name (for bridges are proud), on the other a propaganda, also proudly its opposite, tearing it down. Each foot of the bridge stands in a different reality. Each leg of the bridge is up to its joint in spin, cf. "*traduction* is not translation is not *Übersetzung.*"

This messy bridge contains no discernable kernel of truth. Still, in perpetual war it's our job to pack and unpack the **foil** of Styrofoam and cotton balls, the shredded cheddar . . . To ask, what sort of thing gets packed in so much nonsense? Are we to think it so precious? Or focus on waste and ignore the intended object?

Sun Tzu: "*Hence the use of spies, of whom there are five classes: (1) local spies; (2) inward spies; (3) converted spies; (4) doomed spies; (5) surviving spies. When these five kinds of spy are all at work, none can discover the secret system. This is called 'divine manipulation of the threads.' It is the sovereign's most precious faculty.*"

B knows that his son who crosses the bridge is much better at fakery than anyone else. Evil disguises itself more easily than good, if crossing is the goal.

We were taught:
theories mask actions, so the devil does encourage them.
Novice spies usually seek money.

But a Judas? There are several theories, including:
The "Good Motives Theory" or the "Mixed Motives Theory"—
that either way his betrayal was just poor judgment:
Judas just casting out Romans, or Jesus dilly-dallying.

Any patriot would've done the same.
Some would even call Judas the savior of the
Savior for trying to get him on track.

Judas is heavy packaging. Wad him up and throw him
far away, for the word is gaping, and the bridge
stands undisciplined before us.

It took 28 days, 13,000 meters of rope, and 40,000 m² of
sand-colored polyamide fabric for Christo to dress the oldest bridge in Paris. Does art tell us more about the bridge
than we already knew?

Sun Tzu: "*Hence it is that with none in the whole army are
more intimate relations to be maintained than with spies.
None should be more liberally rewarded. In no other business
should greater secrecy be preserved.*"

You can call her an object, but a bridge cannot be wrapped, encircled, or caught. Her path goes past, in two directions, which doesn't imply a truth. This **impregnable** promiscuity spans obstacles for the purpose of providing passage, even passage as deceiving as false friends, thinking we can speak safely in the middle.

In medias res? Not so much the thick of things as astraddle, watching the course of time. *Sentence, conviction, phrase*—these *faux amis* run their confusion in the smile dressing our faces, our *figures*—while *figures* maneuver from the *pons*, a broadband neural connection bridging hemispheres, implicated in facial expression, sleep paralysis, and the generation of dreams.

On the bridge, we hover in the spot where the flow of wind and water cancel out, a kite skitting first this way, now that, unstable between two pairs of eyes, while considering closing them both in a swift plunge. The bridge, high and tenuous, sways, barely touching the ground as it lifts in a wobbling handstand. We can't make a handshake without revealing the precarious trick. Here the time-bridge suspends, midbrush, free from the ruthless madness, filled with information that is both right and wrong, her head and her hands true and not-true, guilty and innocent.

On one side is B, sighing, on the other, B's son.

> Other Judas theories include the "Direct Request" motive,
> wherein Jesus asks Judas to betray him:
> "I need a friend to hang me as my enemy."

So, pass over, if "over" is what passes. Later, B will search the dark forest with a lamp, to see what was flung off in haste.

Now, we think, with the soldiers sleeping and the land-
mines underfoot, maybe we didn't hear what we heard.
Maybe that bridge, and B's only son, was only a natural accident, the sort of thing that falls across: a tree, some
boulders. Not meant for human travel, just meaningless
noise devoid of purpose.

To capture a bridge, practice distracting guards by starting a fire away from the planned point of entry (falls under
"fire techniques"). Practice climbing a tree and camou-
flaging yourself within the foliage (falls under "wood techniques"). Practice throwing duckweed over water in order
to conceal underwater movement (falls under "water
techniques"). Practice curling into a ball and remaining motionless in order to appear like a stone (falls under
"earth techniques").

Like the theory of Incarnation: if Jesus had God's blood,
then Judas must have Satan's. "Did I myself not choose you,
the Twelve, and yet one of you is a devil?" Can this only
read one way? Bondage reverses obvious power. Toss the
charge directly under the phrase.
It explodes.

A he-spy easily emerges from a she-spy, for there is a cloak the hermaphrodite prefers to embrace beneath, as heroes would jump to lay theirs across a puddle for the damsel's dry-most tiptoeing. **We** is the pronoun *du jour*. It unites family under the sun. Where other pronouns once made slashes, spy intercourse renders all bodies perverse.

Sun Tzu: "*The enemy's spies who have come to spy on us must be sought out, tempted with bribes, led away and comfortably housed. Thus they will become converted spies and available for our service. It is through the information brought by the converted spy that we are able to acquire and employ local and inward spies. It is owing to his information, again, that we can cause the doomed spy to carry false tidings to the enemy. Lastly, it is by his informer that the surviving spy can be used on appointed occasions.*"

Of all important bridge moves, combat engineers know that carrying-blocks of high explosives and a few priming assemblies are enough to make a small demolition kit detonate swiftly. Power possesses both sides of a bridge, not allowing foreigners to face us as we move—or is it that we're on the foreign territory of the friendly facing away . . . ? When a son betrays, is it a treason?

> Judas Puppet Theory:
> He was predestined and had no choice
> (if he would face shame or praise, i.e.,
> "Do not cross the bridge 'til you come to it").

After human tissue is torn open ("a brief fight") the bridges
are up for grabs. "Operation Deadstick" captured the
bridges across the Orne, to move the Allies landing on
Sword Beach toward the enemy in the east. Six Airspeed
Horsa gliders made the "most outstanding flying achieve-
ment of the war." Another glider was the Slingsby Hengist.

> Generation doubles back for gain: Hengist and Horsa
> were Saxon brothers who initiated the
> fifth-century conquest of Britain.

But aren't we rushing to the rail? As though we could ever
gather ourselves for a picture. If they want a bridge, so they
shall have a bridge, and the handlers are helpless to stop us.
If they say no, then what motive drives us, after all, to stare
over at the point of nothing, at the frothing rapids disap-
pearing into a narrow abyss. Sex shifts the rules and they
build up tokens. If he appears as a she, to be sure, someone
wire-hangs in the germ of everything, bungee jumps here
where all direction sags under great pressure to go on.

"Volume from the egg," we whisper in anticipation of
being overheard. "For B exaggerates the drone leash." The
cloaked figure nods and departs.

*That the impact of your army may be like a grindstone dashed
against an egg*—this is effected by the science of weak
points and strong materials.

> Cast out of overpopulated Saxony,

the brothers Hengist and Horsa ("tall strangers in large
ships") landed in Britain and fought for Vortigern, King
of the Britons, in exchange for all of Kent. Hengist and
Horsa then bade more Angles to come, describing "the
worthlessness of the Britons, and the richness of the land."

Will our handler inquire if this bridge was even meant to
be a bridge? Or, why are there so many crossings for this
one small area? Why would the garden of 10,000 bridges
only have five?

At the banquet following a peace accord on Salisbury Plain,
Hengist orders his household to hide a long knife (*seax*)
in the middle of the shoe. The plan was to call out
"*Eu nimet saxas!*" and kill the unarmed Britons
sitting next to them (aka *The Night of the Long Knives*).

We spread more silliness at the bridge's midpoint:
"There may be elephants at the buffet of the first disorder,
viper to the cauldrons of Gaul."

Will nothing ever make political sense
again? Was the voice naked or was it masked?
Did we smile or grimace? Which way were we facing
when we counted silver into a small sack? Failure and
faithfulness both collect fortune.

B asks for his son's accounts.
Gaining is equivalent to stealing.

Consider Creon and Antigone, Roland and Oliver, liege and lady, each justifying nonsense from their own perspective, each eager to lean in for the reward, each ready for a little honey to provide useful *kompromat*, to launder their funds, to break their own off-shore purses.

Insight leads us to riddle around who may approach the bridge, as though all remaining words are mere "chicken feed"—and we've all experienced floods along the banks, the shores submerged and blocked traffic. This is how we find a word in a haystack of pages. Bear it into intelligence.

July 6, 1776:
Thomas Jefferson proposed that one side of the seal
of the new United States feature Hengist and Horsa,
"the Saxon chiefs from whom we claim the honor of being
descended, and whose political principles and form
of government we assumed."

We know a bridge is an obvious family invention, a distraction over a diversion. Lash sticks, lay reed-rope tight. But don't forget the Romans spanned greater distances, for they discovered concrete, by which a military cover-up crosses the nightmares of crowds.

Some questions:

1. Does a water-bridge (so-called because the bridge spans under water) possess the same amount of water beneath it as above it, with the bridge exactly in the middle?

2. Is a bridge a hole? The culvert thinks yes, or maybe not, and the next meeting may take place underground.

In 55 BCE, Caesar's soldiers massacred some Germanic
refugees. Wanting to distract the Senate from the inquiry,
Caesar set off to cross the Rhine and boo the Barbarians
(the Ubians and the Suebians) and, deeming it undignified
to use ships, he devised a bridge (the first on the Rhine),
had it built in ten days, spent eighteen days burning vil-
lages on the far side, and then—"having advanced far
enough to serve both honor and interest"—he cut down
the bridge and returned to Gaul.

Code Names conjure a fleeting romance, or a joke that passes
quickly around a room and disappears. Nationality disappears,
a tribe's women and children, its future, is killed in a code
name, and yet, for the handlers, loyalty is tantamount to a conviction. Nationality is what can be turned against, or worked
for. It is a poison that you can't taste. The war divides nations
into notions, code names conjure clichés.

Brutus-Thumb, the Roman;
Pensée, the Parisian;
Gimme, the American.

It's an imprecise system, but it's all we have. Is the first test
of loyalty where we happen to be born? Suspect border

residents and bilingual speakers: the fatherland? The
mother-tongue? "London Bridge Is Falling Down" and
"Sur le Pont d'Avignon" . . . Scour the children to find
the first tune.

Tension, compression, bending, torsion, and shear—in
all cases, on this bridge, the spy faces a paradox and welcomes an accomplice, of whom we can't be sure. Will a sentence move in a circular direction? Will it be heard as true,
or inside out? The sentence firms up, but straightens in the
mouth as chewed. B's son's sentence is surrounded by other
sentences, themselves crowding in the opposite direction,
just as we oppose our views. B sighs. The future appears.

> Tactical units plunge into the river,
> surfacing downstream as startling platoons.
> The enemy sends dredge-men to sift ore from fay,
> but the rubbly depths only muddy the dregs.
> Water and war conditions retain no constant composition.

> Strike the snake's head and be struck by the tail;
> strike the tail, be bitten by the head.
> Strike the middle and see both ends strike!

Underwater bridges made of logs, sandbags, or piles of dirt get
built just below the surface, to appear invisible while letting
vehicles cross. Air strikes do no harm, for water has distortion
and protective qualities impossible to breach.

> Here are some qualities of a traitor:
> Sneaky, a bit cowardly. Always just below the horizon.
> Even up close, no one sees.

> Second, traitor's luck=magical.
> Conjuring belief from confusion, turning desire
> into facts, fears into truth.
> Other people are just powders to be blended into smoke.

Third=calculating.
Look for the best opportunity to betray,
but make an opportunity
from any encounter.

Four=callous.
This would be the kiss, perhaps one of the
most celebrated of all time.
With a cold heart, say, "Whomever I shall
kiss, He is the one."
And he kissed him, that devil.

Consider the quest: no one's sure what the McGuffin might
be, like the caucus-race in Wonderland, whiling away the
time and leaving us dry. Even handlers and scribes lose
track, passing the grail along the bridge like a hot potato,
pumping the haze but skirting the crux: "*La plus bele rien
que vous onques veïssiez.*"

In these legends the heroes come to a bridge, usually with
a fair tower on the other side. A knight would forbid us
to pass and challenge us to joust. Turning in a blur, we
will smite him.

Variants:
1. the knight is bound with a chain fast about the waist
   unto a pillar of stone;
2. the knight is a lady with a sperhawk on her hand;
3. the knight is a troll who requires you to pay toll (a
   riddle);
4. the knight is lying dead in a great hall; there are three
   pavilions on the bridge, the bridge is a *pont* and a fair
   town full of people are calling *Welcome, Sir Launcelot
   du Lake, the flower of all knighthood*;
5. the knight is your best friend.

> *"Are this you what can't did come thus never fat,*
> *or fail conviction vase and rubber . . . ?"*

And following Caesar by goodly centuries, the Allied air
forces also upped to cross the Rhine, secure the bridges, or
at least not lose both sides at once. The uncaptured bridges at
Nijmegen and Son provided opportunities for Nazis. Bridges
blown up by enemies on departing sowed chaos in a land of
canals, of branches of a river, time tributaries in too many
waters, and few ways to remember. Nazis held their position,
they fed on the failure of the foot that had made the last step
a bridge too far.

That a bridge covers a bed, wet or dry, flawed, still beyond
debate, where children were borne, and triangulating intelligence, in a suspension span, the truth element is distributed
softly in a truss or box beam of lies. But, then again, if it is all
reversed, the wind will continue and the river, too, though
they flow in one direction. Such is life in incipient or covert
wartime.

The judge accuses B's son: If you're born here, maybe you love it
more there, for desire turns heads, or at least splits faces, where
bridges can cross dry stream beds where grout-filled cracks give
only the impression of a stream. Nonetheless, when the river
leaves, the bed remains.

After Caesar's crossing, the Rubicon lost its symbolic
importance as the gate of Rome. Then its course,
deflected by coastal floods, then its name . . .
until only the saying remains.

"Ah, it's you!" isn't uttered straight out. B only sighs at the
absence.

"No, it's you!" sticks, as in all recognition, between the throat
and the eyes. It's my Rubicon, it is the air, after all, that tests
the bridge at the center of the span, and the destruction of the
bridge can make it seem as though it never existed.

Counterintelligence never testifies for either side.

Cutting back, B can't find his son—as with all children who forget to come for dinner and would rather keep playing games in
the mud, even as night requires the heavy toll of their sperhawk,
their three pavilions, their *Welcome, Sir*, and their jousting tower.
Just as B looses a last sigh on the night, his son seems to be dancing with a shadow, a sudden distraction—

How will B pass the sentence?

This is impossible to send by radio, photograph, or fit on the microfilm around a pigeon's ankle. There is no smoke to signal. There is no code concealed in DNA. This has to be "packed in such a way that, opened by an unauthorized person, it would be exposed to the light and so made useless."

Such is the sentence in B's possession.

Maybe temporary and illusory, we think, as if stepping on the unstable deck of a boat, as if we are nothing but France's famously self-destroyed ferry-bridge over the Seine, to slow approaching battalions.

No one can remember why the Perilous Seat must remain vacant at the Round Table. Some say it was Judas's seat; others that it was Christ's, or just Merlin's directive to entice the winner to come forward.

It's been a rainy dawn, with all B's packing and unpacking, with trying to wrangle the sentences to hide their load. Age handicaps. It makes one sharper while hobbling thinking. But what can one age for, except money, when the war takes away every other value at its face? Beauty refuses. It disarms who might fathom it, for it has no truth and turns toxic with the full crush of its emptiness. Desire comes like an army dog, ready to hunt, easily miscued. Come closer for purse or beauty—siren island to the victor.

Was this, back at the office, the spy handler's plan all
along?—not just the beaded pins on a wall map, the miles
of files, neatly cross-referenced to keep track of lines—
but to end up on the Winning Side, which means the side
whose lie gets crossed out. For what human brain can cen-
tralize a joke? Each handler needs a chess player's ability to
plot more than a few riddles, making memories and hind-
sights in real time. Then sound judgment, the ability to call
up figments, two single rows of dominoes wait to fall as we
stare toward our separate shores.

> Would the bridge hang itself?
> That would be illegible; easier said than done.

> In the frozen ninth circle of Hell, the traitors wait.
> Judas, in the company of Brutus and Cassius,
> suffers a few unrelenting torments.

Destroying the Milvian Bridge that crosses the Tiber into Rome,
Maxentius takes a breath and holds back his enemy so he can
keep an eye on them. Who holds Rome, holds the Senate.
Secretly without a glance, he floats pontoon fragments to move
troops both ways. A raft bridge gives safety, but doubles as a
trap, which Maxentius uses to drown Constantine's men.

Standing on the edge of her bluff, her rough hands hold the
future open, trumping those naive enough to believe in luck.
We can teach a lesson in avoiding that mistake.

Our letters remain innocuous, fragmented, almost silly,
as they gather momentum. That's what people read, even
though the ink flows in rivulets detectable to experts possessing the right chemicals, dripping into the water below.
Secret ink couldn't make darkness this unstable. The stars
are match-heads, the water the molecules that reveal glints
and glimmers between the forged iron of moving trestles.

> We pass it on: "*Vile swayback plush, the
> caterwauling up-jam on the son's tail-face.
> Deal to aft or pickle.*"

Our sentences invest an entire world with characters, parties, poetries, news, gossip. We make it all up on the one
hand, and make it real on the other.

> "*Just last night, a bride miracle sang glass au ciel.*"

Did we say we knew B? We never finally met. The bridge
jumps in the windshear of the storm, but rain only tightens
us together. Our little rabbit has lied and knows he knows
it. What backward position can B find that will release this?
A sigh? A flying bridge hasn't yet been made, but it might
lead directly to our reward.

(Nothing is a spy's reward.)

Regards to be sent *poste restante*. B's son has a new cover.

> "—*his coign of vantage, her paste of gain, their play of gaps,
> our profit by breaks, la belle vie far from the front.*"

> Motives come only in theories,
> there is no way to see them.
> One sentence to investigate: that Judas

"falling headlong, he burst open in the middle
and his bowels gushed out." From the height of
the fall, bodies can't stay together.

Reader, decisive bridges are rare. But hey, look again,
and they are everywhere. You think of the capture of the
Ludendorff Bridge left to double-cross, the walking on and
over, the Allies now possessing a direct route to the enemy
heartland. Yes, looking back, the bridge should have been
destroyed.

Like a magician, B's son's absence redirects our eye to
moonlight on all sides of the bridge not there. The river is
loud and that's what you hear. Do not ask what the opposite of "bridge building" is when it comes to traitors, for
they refer to bridges that do not span. Failed bridges are
unholy grails. Do not dare ask.

Now, and forevermore, sift the remaining phrases, pore
over the text looking for a clue packed in others, waiting
to meet itself, to stand its ground. It's what you remember
when questioned, when evil turns to face you.
A sentence was only that bridge that turned around.

Case the Case: 11, rue Larrey

Duchamp: "About the war, there is no significant news.
No important move forward, no move backward.
A hopeless equilibrium."

Paris between doors.

Rrose, are you making two faces? New York between wars?

Subject considered by the discharge board too sick.

Duchamp: "I do not go to New York, I leave Paris. It is alto-
gether different. For a long time and even before the war,
I have disliked this 'artistic life' in which I was involved.
—It is the exact opposite of what I want. So I had tried to
somewhat escape from the artists through the library. Then
during the war, I felt increasingly more incompatible with
this milieu. I absolutely wanted to leave. Where to? New
York was my only choice, because I knew you there. I hope
to be able to avoid an artistic life there, possibly with a job
which would keep me very busy. [. . .] Yet, since you warn
me against New York, if I cannot live there any more than
Paris, I could always come back, or go somewhere else."

Back from New York: "*Une porte ni ouverte ni fermée . . .*"

STUDIO AND DOOR

"*Eau et gaz à tous les étages*" in white on blue enamel. We
are feet among casuals in front of 11, rue Larrey, where our

target lived from 1927 to 1942. Nothing remains of the
studio itself (furniture & woodwork by Duchamp & Man
Ray, plumbing by Pevsner, and, later, a paravent by Jacques
Herold). Behind us, la Grande Mosquée de Paris, a celebrated inauguration in 1926 that was visible from the studio the year Duchamp arrived. The mosque's effort gained
its ground in deference to the 70,000 Muslims who died for
France at Verdun. We think we hear the distant notes of an
organ-grinder: "*À l'arrêt d'la rue Larrey / La mère Larret vend
d'la raie.*"

Reader, we'll start with the obvious: footprints, fingerprints,
hair. We pose, of course, as a *janitor* to gain access.

> Paris between wars: an eerie, notorious, romantic, oblivi-
> ous underbelly of anxiety. Everywhere a Janus looking out
> for themselves in cafés—god-of-doors just re-reading the
> news, or punning for the bartender, ignorant of, or just
> ignoring, the swallow at the *table d'à côté.*

A good reader asks: Did Duchamp marry money instead of
Mary? For six months he nuptialed Lydie Sarazin-Levassor,
half his age and the daughter of a car scion. We've got the
case history: a boxed-in case. They say a fool and his hair
are easily parted. At the notary, Duchamp discovered the
money was short and so then was the marriage.

> "He hates hair," we have her saying. Maybe
> Hair, but not Heiresses.

But for a moment he lived the marriage as any small square
footage, in need of a good carpenter,
>   i.e.,
>   when the door in the studio is
closed, there is one communication, a gray-area:

(communication—O false friends, there's no *false friend*—What do I mean? How do you say, "two rooms communicate"?)

When the bath is closed, the studio and bedroom ***communicate***. When the studio is closed, the bedroom and bath ***communicate***. Or the door—impossible target—can stay open on all sides, compromised.

We have him saying: "*J'ai montré la chose à des amis en leur disant que le proverbe 'Il faut qu'une porte soit ouverte ou fermée' se trouvait ainsi pris en flagrant délit d'inexactitude.*"

Instead of paintings, subject pinned linoleum chessboards to the walls, using medals and decorations for the pieces. When playing a chess game, sketch in air the engine that will win or lose. A pin against the king is *absolute* where pinned pieces cannot legally move, or expose the king to check.

He left a coded note: "*Se raser les yeux
fermés dans son bain. Vérifier la lisseur
avec les doigts. Pas de miroir.*"

We wonder: Did he make some windows fresh, and
others not? A bride is bilingual, two tongues and is she
faithful, in other words, can he ever be married to the
original? What is the object before it is married, *a belle
infidèle*, formal and trimmed to fit a Louis XIV beauty: "*si
elles sont belles, elles sont infidèles; mais si elles sont fidèles,
elles ne sont pas belles.*"

All this leaves us unsure what room remains, and we fear
our communications are busted, even cold. O, how we
long for the quaint uncertainty of a bridge. Mingled and
impure, there's nothing more vertiginous than a choke-
point of architecture, aka "the good old days."

We may have to make a brush pass, full of hair, but here,
an object goes missing right before our eyes. One second we're sure of it, next it's "art." Magicians make things
disappear through misdirection, too: what an eye follows, a brain misses, the rabbit escapes from a hat; rabbit,
mole, ants, bugs—outfoxed and ratted out—what are we,
after all, except walking rules that, when tailed or tailing,
become animals, or at least give that impression.

Our training uses double-blind identity intelligence:
who has the key, has the war—oops—door.

On entering the premises, hair combings should be
taken first, then foreign hairs and fiber samples (we are
not two forces pulling in opposite national directions—
yet we must be prepared for anything behind our backs).
Compared to what we gather, our cover is unimportant.

Make-yourself-at-home: carpenters, janitors, curators. After the "game," one of us will need to redress, sexually, literally, the threshold as a neutral position. Needless to say, if the handlers had run this black-bag job more efficiently, we could re-engage that hovering feeling we've mentioned. But this cover may not hold; we've lost our bridge agent somewhere along the way and the objects have no easy job of it.

> We have it that Duchamp loves fresh heavy windows, like two hairs touching. Duchamp says something about hair that is male-female: "*Il faut mettre la moelle de l'épée dans le poil de l'aimée.*"

For forensics, twenty-five full-length hairs, pulled and combed from different head and pubic regions are needed to track characteristics. Hairs found in the hands belong normally to the victim. But without the subject, contact with interior space causes hair to collect on socks. Doors and windows searched for traces of entry or exit. Package hats in separate paper bags, using care especially with adjustable headbands, as these are a source also for fingerprints: our contamination must be avoided.

> Duchamp: "*Il n'y a pas de solution parce qu'il n'y a pas de problème.*"

> That's fine unless the door acts as its own artwork, an original and its translation, frighteningly linked to borders, hybrids. Covering the scene, can we be sure of proper removal? We feel anxious in this bilingual and punning place. Photograph all evidence prior to touching it; bag each item separately. It's dangerous to let the target out of sight because the eyes change constantly, and lines of sight go both ways. Hiding is blind. Identities make the suspect prime. When every object

doubles, what do we follow? We must prevent change
of portraiture (with a hesitation on the gender);
prime suspects prove odd by definition.

A bicycle wheel, indeed any named and recognizable
cluster function (object), presents an unstable atmosphere, wrapped in informational attributes, not
even a single description-word. They warn us: "If you
sense a fuzzy emanation, you may glean there's been a
recent turning." This isn't grandma's intelligence. Turning
an agent is delicate. Subjects bundle partialities in lied
objects, emotional baggage, preening.

Bicycle Wheel, Paris, 1913. Duchamp: "I enjoyed looking
at it, just as I enjoyed looking at the flames dancing
in a fireplace. It was like having a fireplace in my
studio, the movement of the wheel reminded me
of the movement of flames."

Fresh Widow, 1920, Paris just before
La Bagarre d'Austerlitz.

A bug house can be full of paper ants. This is overheard:
"I'd say I liked the fourth dimension as an
additional dimension in our life."
and
"It was very interesting, this non-Euclidian geometry
put forward by Riemann because there were no
more straight lines. Everything was curved."

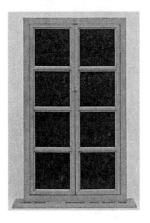

Fresh Widow, 1920.

A door swings to close, but opens instead to a doubled
undecidable space; similarly, the bicycle wheel turns
art, and is found to be only minimally "bicycle wheel."
Ditto "bottle rack" and all recovered objects whose two-
faced agendas place them in this conundrum of locality,
this play of doubling dimensions. The flat is perilously
fixed. On film, a woman's a man looking through cigar
smoke—behind one door a soldier, behind the other a
citizen. Door of wars never close; a slight wasted energy.
Intelligence scattered.

When an agent makes eye contact or becomes themselves
a target, they are said to be "burned."

Later, we learn the smell of an agent
turned is *infrathin*.

FISH-DUEL

In the way the door bifurcates, we could reproduce
asexually if we fancy a fight. The fish who wins the penis-
fencing duel must, for practical purposes, stay a man. The
other slob must give in to the female persuasion, absorb
all the sperm and have some babies. That's deep cover—
and without a head to tail, we must rely on enemies to
stay enemies while knowing:

friends change quick.

Still, we catch messages sent from London to
the Resistance on the radio—it seems this mirror
serves as glass. Shoes deposit hair from a
vehicle to another location.

We know to use *contrepèterie:* so shall we?

For our purposes, the "authentic work of Rrose Sélavy"
provides clusters over time and scale so that conscious

> humans experience only information, hence
> material, the forgery that mocks the art.
> Can he forge this authentically?

> Duchamp wanted a Jewish name for Rrose Sélavy but
> couldn't find a pun-able one; decided to change sex
> instead ("*J'ai voulu changer d'identité et la première idée
> qui m'est venue c'est de prendre un nom juif. [. . .] Je n'ai
> pas trouvé de nom juif qui me plaise ou qui me tente, et
> tout d'un coup j'ai eu une idée: pourquoi ne pas changer
> de sexe! [. . .] Alors, de là est venu le nom de Rrose Sélavy.
> [. . .] Je trouvais très curieux de commencer un mot par
> une consonne double, comme les L dans Lloyd.*")

Double consonants: wasted energy to harness (more
chicken feed).

The sea hare, though a form of snail, has no shell, but
male genitals in front and female behind. The Queen is
a combination of a Rook and a Bishop. Our rabbit uses
"infra-mince" (code name for the smell of swishing swords
or any subtle passage between auras of objects).

> Duchamp: "One of my female friends under a mascu-
> line pseudonym, Richard Mutt, sent in a porcelain uri-
> nal as a sculpture; it was not at all indecent . . ."

Good agents love attention as they hide in plain sight.
Reader, surely, they are right here.

> *Infrathin* gives a pleasurable seam, for instance the
> coatrack nailed to the floor, called "*trébuchet*"—a pun
> on *trébucher* (to trip). Bilingual puns form a blockage,
> being both ugly and unfaithful, jamming interpretators
> from their task. New agents, the interpreter-spies,

pirates and captives, future diplomats,
evolve a bridge language,
lingua franca, to undermine translations entirely.

Two penises emerge from the front of the flatworm like
breasts. A cut, irrationally, doesn't add up, though bachelor operations may. A joke marks physical displacement, a
logical and artistic paradox like the bride-gear planning all
along to be stripped. A joke masks a truth.

Chinese food shows up. We can't know who sent it, but we
think we're marked to be fed. We leave it to some pigeons,
though rats or moles find it first. The first taste of a new
source is often sweet. Poisoned.

Moving occupies two places at different times, so we think
he is where he is not.
Like a suitcase, motion is not a part of him, nor of anything. His "going somewhere" is more an infinite number
of going-nowheres.

Chess is a going-nowhere that can be won.

The person collecting the suspect's items should never be
the same person collecting the victim's. If the same person must be the same person, change clothes and time and
objects cannot be glued together, though they might later
be shimmed.

"Infra-thin separation . . . has the 2 senses
male and female," as we uncover in this "*Objet dard*":

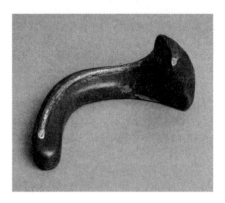

So was Duchamp never/always between
Larrey and Mary's?

TRIBOLOGY-INFRATHIN

Emergency in Favor of Twice, our handler says, "*bring the
objects*!" We look and see a snow shovel. Good example:
we're not sure if we should leave it, or remain sufficiently
indifferent. The potential for conveying information grows
in this new dimension, where noise and dirt and dust
are welcome. Every object says it's a masterpiece, familiar
improvised cover.

> *infrathin: a production which is no longer man-*
> *ual but* coudique *(as in "elbow"). Or L-shaped.*

This mission has objects for object but don't we also seek
evidence, where the target passes into the interval between
identicals? A door swings closed but instead opens unde-
cidably, escaping. Has something passed unnoticed? We try
to imagine how to access the fungible, and luckily there are
specialists—tribologists—who study the science of rub-
bing between faces, exploring *infrathin*. Where a face seems
smooth, a closer look reveals asperities, as the looks diverge
subtlety at the intimate contact where welding takes place.
How is this awkward bottle rack more useful as art and
only somewhat "rack," and ditto now everything else?

> Ditto surfaces whose folded motions stick them in
> conundrums of locality. You look out, while I search the
> premises or scan the box. Museumed in, we think our-
> selves agents of the apartment's perilous fix.

"I want to be alone at home more than every other night." And
one door makes the studio livable.
> Keep in mind that something is
> where nothing might otherwise be.

But we've heard this *infrathin* is the difference between identical things. It's that identity factor that cannot be defined,
but we're told to consider the warmth of a chair recently
abandoned, or the feeling after you've just left the bridge.

Or marry the smell of the mouth and the air that welcomes the
words.

> How we will collect this stuff seems beyond us.

Meanwhile, the woman is a man looking into cigar smoke—leading us to suspect the ultimate asset is not just an "interval" but something that exists opposing forces. Maybe whoever possesses it sees the future as it forms? Even with a key (provided by the landlord) we cannot find a threshold to mark an entrance/exit. Two sides do not cancel but form a third: those "thin films drawn from the outermost surface of things which flit about hither and thither through the air," that Lucretius spoke about. Heat, smoke, dust, mark, print . . .

Materially, an interface, or third body, is a zone of changed composition, a *boîte-en-valise* velocity between solids; these "certified true copies."

Into the air we strain to see a difference that defies measure, we strain to imagine the "cointelligence of contraries" (like the recto and verso of a hollow sheet of paper), "an infinitesimal surface pertaining to two worlds at once."

Basically the handler would be happy with anything, if he would simply say a confused **word**, the one that meant something different in my language, maybe we could move on in yours. Keeping the chain clean is crucial, and free of hair.

An adjustment of half the width of a hair can make all the difference in translation.

But our subject died just as this science of friction emerged, redirecting attention from shapes to surfaces and interfaces—and of course the kinetics of what was once retinal—those interacting surfaces becoming third bodies (children or feelings)—their friction, lubrication and wear.

> God made solids, but surfaces were the work of the Devil, Wolfgang Pauli warned. But surfaces are how objects communicate with the world.

COMB

A painter uses a brush. Duchamp favored the comb.

> There is a **clew** to unravel and it is made of hair. Hair grows but does it live? A hair senses movements of air as well as touch; it can bend the light, forcing a man ray to split (*rendez-vous* with a readymade).

Cf.: his praise for his first wife ("*Elle se coiffe avec un clou*").

French: *traduction*. All language transforms, via the agents, across the border.
English: *translation*. The package remains intact across the border; the agents are invisible.

> A bride to turn around swings on hinges, slides or spins; a double door of two leaves just as a shim ultrathins between objects or a bachelor oscillates. Without the liberty of indifference, a hungry-thirsty donkey dies.*

> Rendez-vous with a readymade. 16 II 16, 11 a.m. The "timing" is the important thing, the "snapshot effect, like a speech delivered on no matter what occasion but at such and such an hour."

> In the case we find only an ordinary metal dog comb— the "original" readymade that survives. It was never stolen

---

* We recall Buridan undercover as a secular cleric, shunning doctrinal disputes:

> "Should two courses be judged equal, then the will cannot break the deadlock, all it can do is to suspend judgment until the circumstances change, and the right course of action is clear."

Duchamp pursued a similar pendular escape, withdrew into chess and finally retracted underground where the ordinary objects he touched lost their use-value. As soon as he embraced one, it changed into a museum piece.

since it was chosen in 1916, and retains its characteristics:
no beauty, no ugliness. Nothing special to notice.

"Classify combs by the number of their teeth," Duchamp
proposed, and while comb-teeth, like bridges, have
harmonic qualities of their own, they are not both
cutouts for the operation.

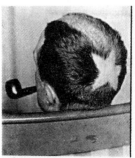

We do find something to bag: Man Ray's photograph, *Tonsure*.
Here the target flaunts a shaved comet (in 1919 or 1921)—the
tail in place of the part.

Man Ray describes Duchamp working and sleeping like a
monk, busy reproducing miniatures of his readymades for his
portable museum, his *boîte-en-valise*.

"I wanted to reproduce them as accurately as possible,"
Duchamp confessed, so we suspect any difference between orig-
inals and *Green Box* models are mere infiltrations.

Before leaving Paris for *la zone libre* and the United States,
Duchamp made an inventory of his ongoing projects. On the
verso he scribbled:

"maid's room
first one after the WC (on the left upon entering)
in the left-hand corner:
1 cylindric pack of Rotoreliefs
1 large box corrugated cardboard of doubles for the
green box
1 pack of faulty reproductions of the malic molds
1 pack of sugar cages printed by Hugnet
1 pack cardboard molding for framing—
all this has nothing to do with the recto of this sheet."

The comet-hair photo reminds us of a 1912 note
included in the green box: "~~Cette~~ Cet enfant-phare
*pourra graphiquement être une comète, qui aurait sa queue
en avant, cette queue étant appendice de l'enfant-phare
~~qui~~, appendice qui absorbe en l'émiettant (poussière d'or,
graphiquement) cette route Jura-Paris.*"

enfant-phare: a headlight-child, a lighthouse-child, a star-
child; sounding *en fanfare*: the flying-start child
to the blast of a brass band; skirting *un
enfant fare* (It.): have/make a child.

Duchamp did not acknowledge his daughter,
Yvonne, born in 1911 to the model Jeanne Serre and later
adopted by her second husband, Henri Mayer. In homage
to her many surfaces, Yvonne became Yo Sermayer. But
Teeny, Duchamp's second wife, immediately recognized
her bona fides and organized a meeting.
We have a recorded encounter in 1966, when our subject
was seventy-nine and the daughter fifty-five:
"I already had two fathers, so I certainly didn't want a third."

It was Aristotle who named the star with hair a *comet*. Was
it Aristotle who also came up with the **bald** syllogism?

(Socrates is bald; Socrates is a man; therefore all men are bald.)

It was definitely Aristotle who said, **"O my friends, there is no friend"**—setting this whole mission off. For Aristotle, ideal friendship meant loving without being loved; while spying is knowing without being known. Just an enemy is a just enemy, who, sharing my back, looks out a different way, and we say we're the best of friends, knowing we're only capable of taking sides.

For double agents, cover is two halves of the partial story. For a bridge agent, the friendship is a half-truth.

Nonetheless, a comet varies according to the exhalation: diffused equally on every side, it is said to be *fringed*; if it stretches in one direction, it is *bearded*. When it moves we seem to have a shooting star. Most comets collect in the Milky Way, but for Duchamp, clouds are shaving lather.

We've had no trouble collecting hairs:

In 1907, a cartoon by Duchamp shows an impatient young woman addressing her beau painstakingly parting his hair, "—*Ce que t'es long à te peigner. —La critique est aisée, mais la raie difficile.*" Criticism is easy but [the p]art is difficult.

"*L'ennemi numéro un est la main de l'artiste.*" ("Enemy Number One is the artist's hand.") He fought it with delay in glass and a *poil dans la main* (French laziness), giving up the palette for the comb (*peigner la girafe*—French pointlessness).

In 1919, subject adds a mustache and goatee to the Mona Lisa:

"the curious thing about that moustache and goatee is that
when you look at it, the Mona Lisa becomes a man. It is
not a woman disguised as a man, it is a real man." Was he
aware that Mona Lisa, as he spelled it, also means thread-
bare pussy in Veneto?
Peindre avec un pinceau à poil.
Is that the crux: painting in the nude / with a brush?
The history of art bristles with nudes painted with animal
hair: Kolinsky sable, squirrel, pony, goat, mongoose or
badger. The finest brushes are made from the male hair
only, but most brushes have a mix of about 60/40 male-
to-female hair. Face recognition software says there is a
60/40 probability that the painting's model was female,
rather than Leonardo in drag.

In 1921, *Baroness Elsa von Freytag-Loringhoven Shaves Her
Pubic Hair.* Some say it was Man Ray's film, others that
it was Duchamp's, and yet others claim it was a three-
way collaboration with the Baroness. Man Ray recalls
helping Duchamp with his research, shooting a sequence
of himself as a barber shaving the pubic hairs of a nude
model, a sequence which was also ruined in the process of
developing and never saw the light.

The Baroness recalls she was "posing as art—aggressive—
virile extraordinary—invigorating—ante-stereotyped."

In 1924, Duchamp issues the *Monte Carlo Bond* or
Obligations pour la Roulette de Monte Carlo showing
Duchamp with his hair and face covered in shaving cream.
In 1924, Duchamp impersonates a Cranachian Adam
with an artificial beard and shaved pubis.

Duchamp: "A painter paints and applies his taste to what
he paints." It's not just that taste is applied with a brush

but that in French, *peindre* (to paint) and *peigner* (to comb)
share the subjunctive form: *que je peigne.*

> *Bête comme un peintre. Sale comme un peigne.*

We zoom in on the comb, hair leaning left or right on
either side of the master-tooth. *Technique à main levée,*
the artist-as-hairdresser firmly draws the part. *Technique
assistée,* combing all the hair back and selecting the groove
that will play the part. Target wore his hair slicked back.
How could he have taken sides when all he wanted was to
remain pat on the part? How can you play with a man who
doesn't want to win and doesn't care to lose?

> In 1923, Duchamp meets Mary Reynolds, a fresh
> war widow, a mechanical equilibrium finely balanced—

> What did you do in Paris between wars?
> Some went on painting.
> Duchamp carried his suitcase around.

MARRY MARY

With Mary Reynolds carrying his case history, it's a
different story, a "hundred years' war," but never *collage* in
the married sense, or *mariage* in the collage sense. Playing
chess to resist commitments: *ni épouser, ni exposer,* in other
words, he would not marry Mary.

> Failing the door, we are then sent for the case, which the
> suspect makes with a box inside, to and fro, as museuming
> begins. Portably. A brush-pass. Hair between floors. Hair
> records time; clues are locked in. Key, then, to what
> someone ate a hundred years ago, what pollution was
> breathed, the groundswell of stress, water and disease.
> But without clear hair, investigation stalls.

Would the bicycle ever have become art except between wars? Would the bottle rack make it back? These double-objects rarely settle, so handlers remain vigilant—which is why at this point we want only the *valise*. He might turn bridge agent to spite us, and pass the models.

We make the most of his tarry with Mary.
He parried Mary, but told her not to be up front about it.
The secret is non-marriage;
Duchamp provides amusing hardware but worries his assets will be uncovered.

Was Mary's but a cover stop? He could see others, but she could not. Unbridled, stripped to her bachelor, a hair-cut or parted, was she bare or playing? He's been seen by everyone with her, but never could she say a word, and we only have his: "the bride is basically a motor."

Hair from a thousand years ago is as fresh as cut off the head.
So we tail the fresh widow to her place on rue Hallé—
secret until it's not, and anyway: stake that out.
Did the target dangle her? Did they use a dead drop?

The paradox of movement of course is that when she exits
the room, she stays in it better than anyone, and outside
like another. But there is a moment when she was leaving,
when she was neither in, also in. Not not-inside, which is a
better way to put it because hairs can be transferred during
physical contact, their presence associates suspects. The
questioned hair is dissimilar to the known hair collected
between Larrey and Mary's. Had he been thinking of
identicals, the most identical castings from the same mold:
"All identicals as / identical as they may be, (and / the more
identical they are) / move toward this / infrathin separative
/ difference."

Chess: a rule-space. Look like you're doing
nothing while in battle.
Darkness at night keeps the bombers ignorant of the city.
One must never light signs or speak bona fides.
Asset more than object, does he object to her "commo"
plan for their punning methods?

Avoiding military involvement, prime numbers factor
nothing except themselves and 1.
We can't identify a prime without personal investigation;
there's an infinite number of them, and no *formula* for
their whereabouts.

Between the wars, Mary's garden grew familiar, with
frequent visitors: Brancusi, Man Ray, Breton, Barnes,
Éluard, Mina Loy, Joyce, Cocteau, and Beckett. At Mary's,
Duchamp papered a wall with maps and studded another

with tacks connected by string. He mapped her house with
lines, but she was the one who stayed in the Paris occupied
by Germans. When Holland fell, Duchamp fled for
Arcachon, southwest of Bordeaux, and then to New York.
Mary remained, maybe because of the cats. This nonsense
stuck Duchamp waiting on the bridge besides, between
sides, recalling her garden and her food. She wasn't
uncomfortable, only hoped to bind the covers of books.

> This was part of her Resistance. (The *portmanteau* will
> double the view. Leave to Remain = Releave.
> To be relieved, released.)
> Think two words and say them at the same time.

"She left her home dressed in ordinary streetwear and went across
the street to a French residence where, an hour later, she saw two
carloads of armed German Gestapo surround her house."
> (Letter from Frank B. Hubachek to
> M. L. Boynton, May 13, 1963)

Hubachek also wrote that Reynolds's home "became the
gathering point and the dispatching point for the spy
poste. It was also a Paris station for the escape route. There
was a continuous procession of individuals, microfilm,
used parachutes, and so on."
> At Mary's, secreted fleeing people hid, and
> collections of information for the Allies, papers
> and documents, lay around in her map-house in
> forged uselessness; treasure-coded.
> She saw how many things hide in a line of sight.
> They knew her as **Gentle Mary**, who sees everything mov-
> ing and says nothing from the front.

> At the last moment she escaped through a sort of double
> door. There's window-doors and door-windows, and

door-doors, and door-walls. We saw them watching her through all these, as a door must finally fold into right and wrong. People caught on the wrong side end up dead.

She crossed the Line of Occupation. The seam. Then needed a guide to cross to Spain. The Germans made firing lines and guides were scarce. Her American accent gave her away and once more she was told never to speak. The simple movement into a new square of even one pawn redraws the power dynamics of the entire board as the shadow bearers work in the infrathin, the whiff of sweat as rook takes pawn, even. The lines having been so meticulously hung across the maps, Duchamp made them string, but she was brave in them.

It is wise to know some pranks one can do with doors. It is wise not to know the destiny of things.

verborum inversiones

Door Pranks (Prank = a practical joke, good for something)
1. Reverse the peephole in a door.
2. Jam coins into the door to prevent anyone from opening it.
3. Tie two door handles on separate doors together.
4. Leave the door slightly ajar and balance a cup of water on top.
5. Remove the hinges and replace the door.
6. Spread tiny threads across the door to make a clear web.
7. Place a "do not enter" sign.
8. Coat the doorknobs with Vaseline.
9. Knock and run.
10. Ring the bell and run.

Mary needed a guide, but her voice was a flare, and yet

> how can a voice be infrathin, and a certified copy too?
> Duchamp had found the language ready-made and gave
> instructions: 1. prepare to say two words, without deciding
> which will be first and 2. say them at the same time.

Duchamp: "*I finally received some good news from Mary
Reynolds—She arrived in Madrid (How??) ten days ago and
she sent a cable to her brother—Yesterday, I received a cable
from her from Lisbon where she hopes to board a Clipper on
January 6. She will be here in a few days if everything goes as
expected—you may not know that she had finally left Paris
and reached Lyon (how??) on September 15. But she failed to
obtain her visa of exit from France before the Germans invaded
the free zone—I thought she was trapped and I feared the con-
centration camp for her (for all the American men and women
are there now)—She will have some stories to tell us!*"

The guides smuggling out of Pau had already been sent
away to the camps; the trains had gone. The Gestapo found
Mary again, and she paid money to walk on foot through
the highest passes of the Pyrénées. Under her arm she carried Man Ray's paintings because she promised she would.

> Finally in New York, she released all her information
> on the Resistance, and on Nazi border-guard
> locations and behavior.

REAL FORGERIES

> After the war, doors no longer but mirrors instead:
> Mirror and reflection = passage from the second
> to the third dimension—three being the Target's
> favorite and final number.

renvoi miroirique

The door at rue Larrey was removed in the 1960s, as
a kind of readymade, and sold and sold again. All the
incriminating hairs would have been swept up, though
the door likely conserved fingerprints of the "*passants con-
sidérables*"—until 1978 when cleaning agents infiltrated
the Venice Biennale and painted it spotless to its owner's
dismay: "*Hanno assassinato la Porta!*"

In Venice it was famous and dirty because hands had lived
through it, but painted over, it's as regular as an old door.

But we follow a rumor that in 1964 Duchamp replaced
the door by a copy and sent the original to New York.

Duchamp:
"*buy or take known
unknown paintings
and sign them with the name of
a known or unknown painter—
the difference between the 'style'* [facture] *and
the unexpected name for the
'experts'—is the authentic work
of Rrose Sélavy, and defies
forgeries*"

Il y a, she says, there is:
the signature (scribbles)
the sound of the signature (LLLLLLLLLL)
the correction (OOOOOOOO)
the orifice of the signature (broken line)
the vibration (wavy line)
the oroxion (more densely broken line)

By the 1940s, Duchamp remained "underground," claim-
ing to have given up art for chess.

In secret for 20 years, subject constructed *Étant donnés* in a tiny studio on West 14th Street, confiding only in three women (two lovers, one wife) and, in the work's later stages, artist/collector William Nelson Copley: "*Nobody had any interest in what he was doing because nobody, including myself, knew he was doing anything. This gave him all the freedom in the world.*"

Needless to say our subject is now in the wind.

Duchamp: "*I was really trying to invent, instead of merely expressing myself. I was never interested in looking at myself in an aesthetic mirror. My intention was always to get away from myself, though I knew perfectly well that I was using myself. Call it a little game between 'I' and 'me.'*"

A Trifle or *Entremet*, for My Better Half, Pending—Being an exchange on the relative benefits of real, spiritual, and logical bridges

Ville d'Avignon interviews candidates for the new city logo

Question*: WHAT is a bridge?*

Pope, seated in full dress with miter and crook—

Pope—I am the Supreme Pontiff, who brought the See to Avignon.

A boy carrying a large stone on his shoulder glances nervously at a flock of sheep trailing him.

Bénézet—I am Bénézet, and angels made me do it; I built that bridge.

Pope's CHORUS—Liar!

Pope—Relax people, it's okay. I hold the keys of Heaven and the power to bind and loose. I am successor of Saint Peter, the rock upon which the Church is built. I am supreme pastor, supreme teacher, and supreme bridge.

Saint Bernard—the *Pontife*, as the etymology indicates, spans between God and man.

CHORUS—When he says "bridge," he means a HOLY bridge not a man-made pile.

Bénézet—Well, Angels said to me: "Kid, ditch those sheep. Build a bridge between man and man." So at the behest of the Lord who bid me to Avignon and gave me the power to lift a great stone, I performed miracles and built a bridge. A real one, over there. Can't you see it?

CHORUS (*holding fingers across their eyes*)—Nope. Looks like a bridge to nowhere.

Pope—I am Pontifex, heir to the *pontifex maximus* through great Caesar.

Bénézet—Well, they're calling me the patron of Avignon, bachelors, and engineers.

CHORUS—Liar!

Pope—Patron by popular fervor, but not a saint. Sorry B, just got word you've been denied canonization in Rome. Your security clearance isn't high enough. Why would God bother with a bridge of stone and wood when he rules over all realms and dimensions throughout time and space?

Bénézet—Bridges signal power, thresholds, transport

between mountains and mountains, between cities and the sea. That could make a desirable association for a Church whose business is limited to the spiritual, but can't get enough of temporal treasure. Look at all those pardoners selling their pardons to the poor whose sins are so small. Call in Petrarch to testify.

Enter Petrarch, exasperated.

Petrarch—Avignon has become the Babylon of the West. The shores of the wild Rhône suggest the hellish streams of Cocytus and Acheron. Everywhere I see men loaded with gold and clad in purple, boasting of the spoils of princes and nations; I hear the lying tongues, and see worthless parchments turned by a leaden seal into nets which are used, in Christ's name, but by the arts of Belial, to catch hordes of unwary Christians.

Bénézet—I bet you the "captivity" of the popes at Avignon will last about the same amount of time as the exile of the Jews in Babylon.

George Dumézil (College de France)—Sorry to intrude, but the *pontifex maximus* is the depositary of sacred science in charge of calendars, invocation formulas, prayers for all circumstances, and the status of different temples. When the good folks in Rome call the *pontifex* a "bridge-builder," they mean "bridge" in its old Indo-European aspect, more like a "path"; its liturgy figured as a path, an itinerary.

Anthony Rich (Caius College, Cambridge)—Actually, the *pontifices* originally referred to those who rebuilt and kept the oldest bridge across the Tiber, the Sublicius bridge, so called because it was built of wood by the king Ancus Martius. Connecting the Janiculum hill to the rest of Rome, the magic of it was that it was rebuilt without nails so that each individual beam could be removed and replaced at pleasure. Yet it was so sacred a bridge that without a sacrifice, no repair could proceed.

Bénézet—Yeah, and do you know that each May the Pontiffs threw thirty mannequins with heels and hands tied up into the river! Who knows if they weren't people before. Is that your legacy: human sacrifice? Pacifying an angry god with human flesh?

Anthony Rich—May I proceed? Beggars begged alms at all hours on the bridge, so the poet Juvenal began calling them *aliquis de ponte*. Gradually, the College of Pontiffs took charge of the religious affairs of the republican city, and the *pontifex maximus* was their first dignitary. Caesar was *pontifex maximus* before he was emperor, so the two roles doubled into one, later translated as: The Pope.

Pope—*Me voilà!*

CHORUS—*Le voilà!*

Bénézet—As a great spy once said: once a bridge is crossed, we leave our old lives behind forever, taking on a new identity. We clean ourselves and we change our clothes and we don't take anything with us.

Pope—The price of loyalty to a cause, my son.

Bénézet—I am not the offspring, but the founder, of the *Fratres Pontifices.*

Buridan—A good example of a false syllogism: Every God is the son, every divine Father is God, therefore every Father is the Son.

Bénézet—After I died exhausted at the age of nineteen, my comrades started *la confrérie de l'œuvre du pont* or *Frères Pontifes*, a bridge-building fraternity of twenty-four monks who continued the work. Besides collecting alms and tolls and building bridges, they looked after ferries and maintained hospices at the chief river crossings.

Pope—Nonsense! The *Fratres Pontifices* is a pure invention of Chateaubriand and other Romantics. Serious historians have shown they never existed. Right guys? A mere legend, a fantasy, no doubt suggested by the *Pontifices* themselves.

Bénézet—But what does it matter, as long as the legend served the bridge-building? It moved people to give alms. My humble origin, my extraordinary calling, people sympathized with me. Like Joanne of Arc, I was shepherding when I heard the Lord summon me. Like Percival, I was the lonely child of a widowed mother called on to an extraordinary destiny by an apparition. Like Cyrus, Mithridate, Eupator, Artaxerxès, the greatest Iranian kings, I was raised secretly with shepherds. An angel disguised

as a pilgrim carrying a stick and a beggar's bag showed
me the way from Vivarais to the Rhône, and I was awed
by the width of this great river. Where any self-respecting
medieval chevalier comes to a bridge, a *gué*, a perilous passage, I didn't find a bridge, just water hundreds of meters
across. They say I played John the Baptist, floating into
Avignon the ancient way, ferried by a Jew.

"Find the Bishop!" someone yelled, and I found him
preaching in the cathedral. Their laughs ricocheted against
the vaults when I told them the Lord had sent me to build
a bridge across the Rhône. The Bishop threatened to have
me flayed and my feet and hands cut, like a criminal. And
when I told the Provost the Lord had sent me to build a
bridge across the Rhône, he roared: "What! you are the
lowliest of men and you own nothing and you boast you
will build a bridge across the Rhône where neither God,
nor Saint Peter, nor Saint Paul, nor Charlemagne himself, nor anyone else succeeded! Since a bridge is made of
stones and mortar, I will give you a stone in my palace; if
you can move and carry it, I will believe you can build this
bridge."

So, putting my trust in the Lord, I took the stone, so
heavy that thirty men could not have moved and carried
it, and set it down at the foot of the bridge as though
it were a pebble. The Provost kissed my hands and feet,
offering me 300 sous, and the crowd was awestruck and
confessed the Lord is great and powerful. And then I was
given 5,000 sous.

After that, my miraculous strength vanished, so I
specialized in fund-raising, an equally formidable task!
I traveled up and down the various provinces to collect
alms. Refusing the honor of being buried in Notre-Dame
des Doms, I received a small chapel on the bridge, which
quickly became a place of worship for pilgrims, and the
money continues to pile up.

Pope—Each time I cross the river, I make a donation of one florin.

CHORUS—Yes, he does!

Question: *WHAT is a lie?*
A statement known to be false by a speaker.
A person to hear the statement, believing it to be true, or not.
Across the truth the lie bridges.

I disagree. One can lie without saying a word.
Also, a speaker can say something perfectly true and still intend to deceive.
And there doesn't have to be a person hearing the state-ment, or even oneself. One can lie to an eavesdropper.
Finally, I can say there are no saints to someone who is a saint and it can be false but I intend the hearer to believe I think it's true.

Okay then, what about a double-insincerity, where a speaker insincerely says something and insincerely means it to be believed. It's the liee's false belief in the sincerity of the liar that creates the bridge that might lead to harm or reduced liberty of judgment. Saying there is no bridge along that path, just to save the lives of a battalion because you know the bridge to be booby-trapped, is nevertheless a lie.

Bénézet—It is the nature of a drawbridge, like the first one built at Babylon, to be pulled up at night so that the inhabitants of one shore cannot loot and vandalize the other. I did not build a drawbridge, though there is the Pope and there is the French King. There is Avignon and there is Rome. Between all things there is no trust. No one trusts a bridge with half its feet on the ground.

Earl of Arundel—And this, if I may interject, is why I'm constantly in the forced company of certain French chevaliers, even after I was "translated to become Bishop of St. Andrews" . . . No one passes between England and Avignon without being considered a spy, though letters of safe conduct ensure our lives, and the chevaliers our silence.

CHORUS—It was the Black Death that followed you!

Pope—O yes, awful! I canceled everything and hid in my room for three months, as envoys continued to cross between England and the Curia.

CHORUS—Messenger, Knight, Diplomat, Spy!

Bénézet—They say the ANTI-POPES are in Avignon.

Enter a Franciscan, robes in tatters, aiming a finger at the Pope.

William of Ockham—You may charge me with apostasy, but I charge YOU with seventy errors and seven heresies, including abandoning the doctrine of Apostolic poverty!

CHORUS—Liar!

Pope John XXII—You've been treated well here, there's no need for all this bluster. If you continue, I'll excommunicate you without a second glance.

William of Ockham—My poverty, the poverty of Jesus and Saint Francis, has been offended by your ill-begotten opulence and unfettered materialism. It's not enough for my philosophy to try to connect what cannot be connected (for I only believe in individuals by their own right and reality, and not metaphysical universals) these two realms are unbridgeable except in words and minds. If God wants to become a person, he will cross the divide. He'll become a goat or a stone. He'll do what he wants to join reality.

Pope John XXII—Now that's just crazy talk.

CHORUS—Crazy!

Petrarch stands up from a corner, wringing his hands.

Petrarch—No, he's right. Avignon has become the Babylon of the West. Instead of holy solitude we find a criminal host and crowds of the most infamous satellites; instead of soberness, licentious banquets; instead of pious pilgrimages, preternatural and foul sloth; instead of the bare feet of the apostles, the snowy coursers of brigands fly past us, the horses decked in gold and fed on gold, soon to be shod with gold, if the Lord does not check this slavish luxury. In short, we seem to be among the kings of the Persians or Parthians.

Ockham sticks a finger toward the Anti-Pope, stirring the air.

William of Ockham—For me to call you a heretic, it's not enough that you've committed heresy, you must have held to it *stubbornly*, even after it's been shown to be false. You, Pope, have written anti-poverty decrees that include "a great many things that are heretical, erroneous, silly, ridiculous, fantastic, insane, and defamatory, contrary and likewise plainly adverse to orthodox faith, good morals, natural reason, certain experience, and fraternal charity." You are not a real pope, you are a pseudo-pope, a lie-pope, and you must be removed and stopped of your pontificating!

CHORUS—Blasphemy!

William of Ockham—*Numquam ponenda est plualitas sine necessitate.*

> *A company of Routiers, under the leadership of Arnaud de Cervole, descends along the Rhône, sacking the Pont-Saint-Esprit above Avignon. They who control the bridge control God and commerce. The Pope is blockaded, the city may starve. But the Plague comes up the other shore, and the bridge is abandoned by the terrified bandits.*

Black Death—I am worse than a house fly that so stealthily torments.

WHAT is a fly spy?

Earl of Arundel—There was no truce at this time, or peace, between England and France, and my messengers visiting Avignon were ambushed on their return. Why would an Empire as strong as Rome resort to the petty criminality of espionage? Make no mistake, intelligence operations are as old as civilization. A man behind a curtain, overhearing, is

enough to get things started. Yet information is not intelligence, there must be a target, and the product of intelligence from the target is action. Caesar used codes and
ciphers and his network of *courriers* and eavesdroppers to
keep his plans private. After Caesar, the reliance on this private messenger system gave way to the *cursus publicus*, a state
road and information highway.

Plutarch—But shouldn't words be secret? Even the Delphi
oracles keep their records in secret scripts, and the great
Cleopatra's tongue "was like an instrument of many strings
she could turn to any language she pleased . . ." Aren't words
and power always corrupting?

Anti-Pope, Clement VII—I've got in my hands the
Liber Zifrarum, the Book of Ciphers, showing how to use
short groups of letters for proper names when writing an
encrypted message! What a clever secretary, my Gabriel
di Lavinde, to bring such a thing to Avignon! Codes are
for words, but ciphers are for letters. Mixing the two, as
my Secretary has done, is a blessing called a *nomenclator*.
One word stands for a place or a person, another word for
another. Whole sentences are code for entirely different
sentences! To an initiate, what seems like a simple idea

about what herb to plant in the garden, conveys where the enemy is at camp to an undercover agent. Having a bilingual dictionary of code words helps.

Petrarch—Avignon is the filthiest and most foul-smelling city on earth. That lousy bridge is the only fixed crossing between Lyon and the Mediterranean, and the only route between the Pope's Comtat and France of the Kings. Everyone's on edge about it, guarding their side. Makes for an unhappy day, I'll tell you. As a tourist, I prefer the pleasure of the trees and fields, and to climb what no one's climbed: that Windy old Giant, Mount Ventoux . . .

Buridan—Oh, pssshaw, I climbed that just last year! And I survived a river drowning by the King, hitting a Pope's head with a shoe, and losing my career in Paris for my philosophical views!

CHORUS—Liar!

Buridan—Any thinking person will agree that what's true is true, what's false is false, but then there's everything in between that we can't know because it hasn't happened or is speculative or made-up or just plain unclear. Add to that the fact that only what's true *right now* is really true, and you'll have to agree that to study philosophy is to study what one experiences in life and thinks in one's mind, not what is mysteriously revealed on the faith of scripture. Theology is never knowledge.

Petrarch—Avignon will be left only half a bridge. Can that be true?

Buridan—Depends . . . Is half a bridge still a bridge?

Petrarch—Is half an allegory still an allegory? Is halfway up a mountain also halfway down?

Buridan—Consider sophism #17: Socrates wants to cross a bridge but it's guarded by Plato.

Plato says, "Socrates, if the first thing you say is true, you can cross. If it's false, I will dump you in the water."

Socrates says, "You will dump me in the water."

Petrarch—So, is that true or false?

Buridan—Exactly.

>*Under cover of night, the liars and friars and saints and popes flee Avignon.*

>*A loud braying in the distance. As they approach, they come to a river swarming with donkeys. A bizarre fixture spans the river. There is a warning sign: Pons Asinorum ahead.*

Pope—Aha! If you like rock climbing and Mont Ventoux's no match, why don't you try the *Pons Asinorum*? Our friend Richard de Bury compared it to a steep cliff that no ladder may help scale.

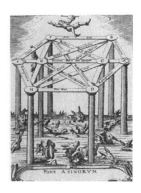

PONS ASINORVM.

Petrarch—That rascal's no friend! When we met in Avignon, he impressed me favorably as not ignorant of literature and curious beyond belief of hidden things, but he never kept the promise that he would fill me in on the isle of Thule after he returned to England, and he never answered my letters. O friend, there is no friend!

Someone—I thought it was the *Elefuga* that Richard de Bury compared to a cliff . . .

West & Thomson—It's the same thing: both *Elefuga* and *Pons Asinorum* refer to the fifth proposition of the first book of Euclid, the theorem of isosceles triangles—that the two base angles of an isosceles triangle are equal.

Someone Else—Well, this raises the question of symmetry, which is a kind of self-congruence, two sides of the same coin . . . The test to show the theorem as operationally self-evident would therefore be to copy the triangle in a turned-over form and verify that it fits with the original.

West & Thomson—*Elefuga* is Roger Bacon's name for the *Pons Asinorum*, fancifully derived from *fuga elegia*, the flight of the wretches—or *flemyng of wreches* in Chaucer's words. That proposition was the terror of novice geometers.

Someone—Except Chaucer applies *flemyng of wreches* not to *Elefuga* but to *Dulcarnon*, a term loosely applied to any dilemma ["to be at dulcarnon"] and properly applied to the two-horned forty-seventh proposition of the first book of Euclid, so named from the sticking up of the two smaller squares at the top of the figure used in the old manuscript geometries.

West & Thomson—Yes . . . Euclid's fifth proposition is
the first test in the *Elements*, testing the intelligence of
the reader and working as a bridge to the harder proposi-
tions that follow. See how the diagram resembles an actual
bridge?

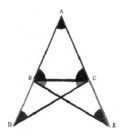

Someone—Pardon me? A donkey's head, *à la rigueur*. Or
a dunce cap.

Pope—Had you seen the Devil's Bridge, you'd know some
bridges are blunt, if not sharp.

Ockham—If I may: the bridge of asses crossed over to
mathematics but originated in logic where it designates a
scheme for exhibiting the finding of the middle term by a
diagram, a matter greatly advanced by my pupil Buridan.

Buridan—Indeed! I established a *certa regula* for finding
the middle term, which is called the *pons asinorum*, an *ars*
for finding the syllogistic middle term, or a *modus* of showing in general how extremes disjoined by negation are to
be copulated; and it is called the *pons*, because the extremes
separated by negation are united as the banks of a river are
joined by a bridge. It is likewise called the *pons asinorum*
because those who are skilled in the art of logic are thus
separated from the dullards.

Ockham—See his *De Asino*, sadly lost.

> *Some dullards grow restless in the court, stomping*
> *and coughing . . .*

Buridan—In it I also expounded on the ass standing midway between equally attractive bundles of hay, and in danger of perishing from hunger, either by reason of his impotent or his equally balanced will.

Tartaretus—So that the art of finding the middle term may be easy and clear to all, I appended the following figure. The nonce-words inscribed on the planks of the bridge are mnemonics for the nineteen valid combinations of the three figures of the syllogism with premises of different strength. Any dunce will find his way across . . .

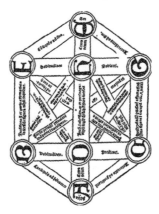

Someone— . . . and go round in circles. This confirms my worst misgivings. All of scholastic logic is asinine. It is dubious whether the asses are those who fail to negotiate the *pons asinorum*, or those who bother with it in the first place.

Tarteret—No let me explain, it's quite simple:

> *. . . chanting as the others escape and risk the bridge amidst the braying.*

E's the subject, F its sequent, G precedent, F outside;
A's the predicate, B its sequent, C precedent, F outside . . .

> *Pope trips and falls in the water, per accidens. His miter floats downstream.*

To conclude to a universal affirmative, a middle is to be taken which is sequent to the subject and antecedent to the predicate; and this is shown by *Fenaca* . . .
To conclude a particular affirmative in *Darapti*, *Disamis* and *Datisi*, a middle is to be taken which is antecedent to both extremes, as is made clear by *Cageti* . . .

> *The bridge is collapsing. All swim with asses and dullards in nineteen valid combinations and three figures.*

To conclude to a universal negative in *Celarent* or *Cesare* a middle is to be taken which is extraneous to the predicate and consequent on the subject, as is made clear by *Dafenes*.

> *The Chorus plays tennis and smokes.*

But if the inference is to be in *Camestres*, the middle must be extraneous to the subject and consequent on the predicate, as is made clear by *Hebare* . . .

> *They scramble up the opposite riverbank clawing at the mud.*

To conclude indirectly to a particular affirmative, the

middle must be antecedent to the subject and consequent on the predicate, as is made clear by *Gebali*.

All together chant the nonsense dunce-words.

Barbara, Celarent, Darii, Ferioque prioris
Cesare, Camestres, Festino, Baroco secundae
Tertia grande sonans recitat Darapti, Felapton
Disamis, Datisi, Bocardo, Ferison. Quartae
Sunt Bamalip, Calames, Dimatis, Fesapo, Fresison.

*NB: Each word is to be taken as the formula
of a valid mood.*

~~Monster~~ Between the Coldest Us

After the Great War, new neighbors ask: Which war?
The great one, the one just starting.

Flip.

Assigned to the movie palace, can we be any more out
of place?
Bald-faced, bare-faced, facing the music, are we so
new and innocent?
Between the wars, can we endure more elusive covers?

After the Great War, Judas makes a comeback in a number
of French novels, no longer as the arch-villain wielded by
ecclesiastical anti-Semitism, but as a more nuanced figure.
Now his treason is a sort of deeper truthfulness towards
his friend, and toward his friend's real or imagined destiny.

Flip.

Suss me out; a surface tension of us/them suspicion,
turning Technicolor, turning off the evening news.

Why do you distrust me? Aren't we friends?
                    I try to turn, but turning, turn you.

After the Great War, this was the nightmare of all double
agents: they were unloved children stuffed into a van and
told to hold their noise down (or else!) while their parents
enjoyed a moonlight fling.

(Which war?) The last one. The next one. The great one.
Yes, my dears, goodnight kiss, go back to sleep—

No one is out there;
Nothing is as it appears.
(How can you not believe me?)
If I say it, you can take it as true.

Are monsters always monsters under cover?
What about Santa Claus?
Consider:

1. He comes at night (~~communist atheist~~)
2. handing out toys (~~consumerist materialist capitalist~~)
3. Exploiting desire

Should we continue to celebrate this guileless agent of gifts?

> Children ask: "How could you lie to me?"

Senator Margaret Chase Smith to a Hoey Committee witness, on the security risks posed by ~~homosexuals~~ Santas in government:

> "Isn't there a quick test like an X-ray
> that discloses these things?"

(Which war are we discussing again?)

A brass band crosses the intersection, holding up traffic.
Patriots stand and salute. We line up for our Loyalty Oath.

> *"Like most of my generation, I was obsessed by a complex of terrors and longings connected with the idea 'War'; 'War,' in this purely neurotic sense, meant The Test. The test of your courage, of your maturity, of your sexual prowess: 'Are you really a Man?'"*
>
> (Christopher Isherwood)

> Approaching the movie palace, can we coordinate
> intelligence?
> Saving face, are we so odd?
> Between the wars, do I turn the other cheek?
> Between the wars, will you keep an eye out?

> "The problem is entirely different since the cold war
> started. Before, treason was a matter of corruption, or
> grievance, or mental instability. Today Marxist faith
> has proved capable of subverting men otherwise of

upright character and balanced mind. How are they to
be detected in time to save the country from them, and
them from themselves?"
(Daily Telegraph, 1955)

We have been tailing a crowd of Santas.
Half went toward the beach, the other half into a matinee.
Wearing dark glasses, they pay their entrance.
Some give you the nod as they go in, so you turn to me in
surprise, and I turn back to put you in the line of sight.

"A curious freemasonry exists among underground
workers and sympathizers. They can identify each other
(and be identified by their enemies) on casual meeting by
the use of certain phrases, the names of certain friends, by
certain enthusiasms and certain silences. It is reminiscent
of nothing so much as the famous scene in Proust where
the Baron de Charlus and the tailor Jupien suddenly
recognize their common corruption."
(Arthur Schlesinger Jr., *Vital Center*, 1949)

(Have we been made?)

"If a person consistently reads and advocates the views
expressed in a ~~Communist~~ Santa publication, he may be
a ~~Communist~~ Santa. If a person defends the activities of
~~Communist~~ Santa nations while consistently attacking
the domestic and foreign policies of the United States, she
may be a ~~Communist~~ Santa. . . . If a person does all these
things, over a period of time, he MUST be a ~~Communist~~
Santa! But there are other ~~Communists~~ Santas who don't
show their real faces—who work more—silently." ("How
To Spot A ~~Communist~~ Santa: Armed Forces Information
Film Number 5," MCML)

One of us is sent out to infiltrate the tomatoes at a campfire, eventually blowing cover while eating a hamburger and asking if anyone could "pass the ketchup."

In May, 1942, Radio Paris vindicated the law ordering ~~Jews~~ Santas to wear an identifying yellow star by the fact that they didn't have "blue skin."

"Le mal vient de ce que les Français, dans leur grande partie, ne savent pas reconnaître les Pères Noëls ~~Juifs~~. S'ils le savaient, ils se tiendraient sur leurs gardes. Donc la question ne se poserait pas si, par exemple, les Pères Noëls ~~Juifs~~ avaient la peau bleue. Mais ce n'est pas le cas. Il faut donc qu'on puisse les reconnaître."
(Charles Laville, Radio Paris, 1942)

"This article is for your protection.
Read it—and be better able to judge the men you
THINK you know!"
(Wally Levine, "The Ways to Spot a ~~Homosexual~~ Santa,"
1956)

We take a pause to reflect on the so-called intelligence.

Q: So why is it okay to lie to children that Santa Claus is real?

A: Because eventually they'll figure it out using their burgeon-
ing rational minds.

Q: But then won't they know that the people they trusted
most have lied to them for years?

A: It's a good lie; it's fun; it's for the kids' benefit.

Q: But doesn't a lie stifle imagination and encourage blind
credulity?

A: While killing the joy of something benign is just cruel.

"They are out to infiltrate all-male institutions like the Army
and Navy, boys' schools, and deliberately ensnare 'candidates'
to join the fraternity . . . Decoys are widespread in these
places, whose 'mission' is to get a borderline case into the
fraternity, by seducing him and forcing him to join once he
has been compromised. . . . today it is far more than just a
perversion. It is a veritable conspiracy." (Jerome Adams, "Are
~~Homosexuals~~ Santas a Hidden Menace," 1958)

> *He sees you when you're sleeping*
> *He knows when you're awake*
> *He knows if you've been bad or good*
> *So be good for goodness' sake!*

Paranoia sees itself everywhere, a Janus-case of newspeak:

Traitors and deviants cannot be identified—(But must!)

They are freaks—(Of an all-too-common sort!)

They are everywhere—(Yet must be quarantined!)

Evil is genetic—(But may be contagious!)

GENE OR GERM?

"~~Communism~~ Santa is a virus that cannot be detected by any security microscope: screening will only tend to exclude those who have avowed themselves Santas ~~Communists~~—not now the most dangerous strain." (*Spectator*, 1955)

"One ~~homosexual~~ Santa can pollute a Government office."
(Hoey Committee)

"The body politic, like the (male) body, establishes its integrity by maintaining its impenetrability." (Cameron McFarlane)

"An open society has been unable to defend itself against a secret society which has formed in its midst. That, when it happens to the cells of our body, is called a case of cancer, and the results were cancerous in their corrupting painfulness."
(Rebecca West, 1964)

". . . any penetration, however slight, is sufficient to complete the crime specified in this section." (District of Columbia Sodomy Laws, June 9, 1948, 62 Stat. 347, ch. 428, title I, § 104; 1973 Ed., § 22-3502)

"Its political action is a fluid stream which moves constantly, wherever it is permitted to move, toward a given goal. Its main concern is to make sure that it has filled every nook and cranny available to it in the basin of world power." (George Kennan, "The Sources of ~~Soviet~~ Santa Conduct," 1947)

"IS THERE SUCH A THING AS A ~~HOMOSEXUAL~~ SANTA FIVE-YEAR PLAN?"

"O my friends, there is no friend."

Flip.

> You turn to catch my eye and, in turning,
> turn me again, getting dizzier.
> Heads or tails? We flip a two-headed coin.
> We cannot seem to win.
> We are stuck in a game of chaos.

They assign us a bridge, but an earth to turn around?
A natural satellite; but is the moon Earth's friend?

Distracting ourselves we flip to keep blurry, to stay dizzy.

> "An open society can tolerate many secret societies. It
> depends on the kind they are. They are dangerous only when
> controlled by a foreign power dedicated to the destruction of
> a free society." (Sidney Hook, 1964)

> We stumble into the theater palace, gumshoe floors,
> literally, blindly sprawl across two seats midway,
> positioning our double face to alternate toward the
> screen. Remove my scarf, shed your coat,
> within our head a split nucleus—a cold
> night for monsters, a hot one for Santas,
> and not just at the movies.
> We try to imagine the horror resolved to
> grease paint and rubber cement, but the beards and

> tufts and facial hair in all the wrong places mark
> insanity, or the truly not-human
> (—the ~~agent~~ Santa in the mirror?)

The matinee has all kinds of ~~monsters~~ Santas in a variety of covers.

By Christmas there are thousands on the boulevard. We have
tailed one away from the theater, away from the crowd.

> We are told: all four ~~spies~~ Santas are alike in that their educa-
> tional backgrounds reflect an unusual lack of contact with the
> liberal arts disciplines.

"Professor Blunt's treason and duplicity do pose fundamental
questions about the nature of intellectual-academic obsession,
about the co-existence within a single sensibility of utmost
truth and falsehood, and about certain germs of the inhuman
planted, as it were, at the very roots of excellence in our
society . . . a man who in the morning teaches his students
that a false attribution of a Watteau drawing or an inaccurate
transcription of a fourteenth-century epigraph is a sin
against the spirit, and in the afternoon or evening transmits
to the agents of Soviet intelligence classified, perhaps vital,
information given to him in sworn trust by his countrymen
and intimate colleagues. What are the sources of such scission?
How does the spirit mask itself?" (George Steiner)

What prompted Beat fellow-traveler John Clellon Holmes
and ~~gay~~-Santa nightclub owner Jay Landesman to morph
into two-headed author Alfred Towne and to castigate a
~~homosexual~~ Santa "coterie" for permeating quality fiction
and Hollywood screenwriting and imposing a "new taste"?
"Long practiced in unraveling symbolism and allusion,"
they claimed, "this 'fifth column' threatens a gradual
effeminization of artistic and sexual values."

Turns out there are at least two hundred more Santas milling around the cinema. We have been made in being unmade, a perfect strike-thru of movie monsters and comic book heros. The ones who have done the leaking are now out in the cold, and we will never have the rights to reproduce their likenesses.

By day's end we've covered the movie palace: we've bugged it high to hell—we hear everything:

Walls pox, insulated contra vibration. Transmitters dig in the pores of the joint. The windows, the cushions, the carpets, magazines in our hands, these are Trojan Horses and armies of extras, infrared film pictures that need no natural, even visible, light. There are bugs in the sewer, the drain pipes, the chair rails, and the quick plant bugs we bump on you in passing, or lay on your coat. Our coats have buttonholes we squeeze to shutter you when you smile and run to us so unnervingly. Our watches, our cigarettes, our wallets and lipstick, everything infrathin and ready-made— an audience full of ~~Santas~~, and all that's playing is a short reel of Cardinal Richelieu's cabinet noir; ancient parry and thrust—king's spymaster says: "friends always listen in on friends," and hands him a block of code;

a long list of faux-amis

"There exists in the cabinet noir of a certain German prince, a book compiled by the Secret Service from the reports of German agents who have infested this country for the past 20 years, agents so vile and spreading debauchery of such a lasciviousness as only German minds could conceive and German bodies execute. . . . for the propagation of evils which all decent men thought had perished in Sodom and Lesbia . . . the names of 47,000 English men and women . . . Privy Councilors, youths of

the chorus, wives of Cabinet Ministers, dancing girls, even
Cabinet Ministers themselves, while diplomats, poets,
bankers, editors, newspaper proprietors and members of
His Majesty's household follow each other with no order
of precedence . . . Wives of men in supreme positions were
entangled . . . In lesbian ecstasy the most sacred secrets of
State were betrayed." (Captain Harold Spencer,
"The First 47,000," *The Imperialist*, 1918)

"When the blond beast is an ~~urning~~ Santa, he commands
the ~~urnings~~ Santas in other lands. They are moles. They bur-
row. They plot. They are hardest at work when they are most
silent. Britain is only safe when her statesmen are family men."
(Arnold White, 1917)

During the lavender scare, the legend of the *Black Book* revives:

This time, the Nazis compile lists of ~~homosexuals~~ Santas and
these lists are supposedly seized by the Soviets when Berlin
surrenders in 1945, and now the ~~Communists~~ Santas use the
lists, again dubbed the "Black Book," to identify blackmail
targets worldwide. This is not to be confused with the Black
Book listing 2,280 prominent British and International people to be immediately taken captive and killed should the Nazis
prevail in England. This is not to be confused with the Black
List of communist sympathizers brought before the House
Un-American Activities Committee.

The trail of a monster grows colder the closer we get,
so we maintain a distance of description when an
image would have traveled twice as far as fast.

"Another reason for the ~~homosexual-Communist~~ Santa
alliance is the instability and passion for intrigue for
intrigue's sake, which is inherent in the ~~homosexual~~ Santa

personality. A third reason is the social promiscuity within the ~~homosexual~~ Santa minority and the fusion it effects between upperclass and proletarian corruption." (Countess Rosa Goldschmidt von Waldeck, "~~Homosexual~~ Santa International")

SAME BOOK, DIFFERENT COVERS

Later, in our Chinese restaurant in Paris, we review our current suspicions, the many intelligence reports, and all our false friends:

abus is simply misuse; *actuel* is happening but not real; *avertissement* warns but doesn't sell; the *affluent* leads to a river not a rich life; *assister à* means to be there but not help, while *attend* is to be there but not wait; *assorti* matches, does not differ; you can put your money in a bank or on a *banc*; a *déception* is for one a disappointment, for the other, a lie; and *demander* asks with or without force; *eclipser*, to slip away or cover; *haïr* to hate, or just hate hair; *hâte* is haste or hate like *haïr*; and a *pair* is someone equal, not a double; *se presser* is to hurry not just to push; *rejeton* is one's child, not the rejected; *sinistre* may just be a mood not a menace; your *sort* is your fate and your type:

Flip—

when you freak out, *je flippe*

flip my wig or flap a wing

When your slip shows
I hold my brief in shorts
When you go straight, I feel *gauche*
When you're *à l'ouest*, I feel adroit

> So let's share a *casquette*
> till death do us part
Let's split a *boulette*
And we can spare an *arme*
> Let's share a *blanquette*
> Let's split a piece of *pain*
Lend me your *faux-amis*
and you can use my falsies
> Please hold my *main*
> until *demain*

We walk out tentative and teetering, like perfect question marks.

How to become a ~~monster~~ Santa:

> walk stiffly, talking in accents, wearing disguise and
lurking, misunderstood by the corner under a streetlamp. To
get your face just right: imagine you smell something sweet
but cannot smile. Fluff your hair. Slick your hair. Jutt the chin.
Suck in the cheeks. Peer to the side. Squint. Stare. Have we
reached a thousand faces yet?

When was Peter Lorre, with his accent and "double-take job,"
ever not cast as the sinister foreigner after he fled Germany and
made it to Hollywood? After his career with Brecht and Lang,
he was cast as Quasimodo, Dr. Einstein, Baron Ikito, Doctor

Gogol, Montresor, Le Chiffre, *Mr. Moto Takes a Vacation,*
Japanese detective-spy, secret agent, son of Frankenstein,
occasionally co-starring with Bela and Boris.

"You know, Rick, I have many a friend in Casablanca, but
somehow, just because you despise me, you are the only
one I trust."

> *"If I had to choose between betraying my country and my
> friend, I hope I should have the guts to betray my country."*
> (E. M. Forster, 1939)

> *Les bras ballants*—swinging arms empty handed
toward the *hôte*, both host and distinguished guest
> > *"Tu me manques"* you miss me, but I miss you
> > *Le temps révolu* has not come round again
> > though we maybe *fell in the apples*
> > in this *déception sentimentale* . . .

> (Newsreel: standard images of suffering, trains,
soldiers, zeppelins)
> > Soviets cut off half of Berlin,
> > blocking a road and a train route
> > (Newsreel: a world anxiously watching)

> Until a wall cements the border, and feature films
on the western side of town become popular destinations for
regular people from the east, who would risk arrest for an
evening's entertainment?

Chess, such as it is, grows more obsolete and the planet
watches, even as players hurry to switch sides.

> Propaganda: inside the theater, the bloodless attack
of images and plots—a view of an alternative world: people on

one side of the wall appear human but have superpowers the other side doesn't. This is seductive. This is new weaponry. Soft weaponry: a fantasy world (false news) *Une nuit blanche*? Sleep my dear. Trust the translation: here a big cheese is *une grosse légume*, and a change of heart is *changer votre fusil d'épaule*. We all translate and double-cross the bridge when we come to it (*chaque chose en son temps*) whether we call it a *split* personality or a *double*. *Une chape de plomb*.

Meanwhile, in New York, Marcel Duchamp reveals his pun on the Brooklyn Bridge (pont iff)—and accuses America's art of being nothing but plumbing and bridges.

IN RE MULTIVERSE

After the great war:
the multiverse starts.
And our time arrives like a train back at the station, pulling much more than its original weight, though it is empty and possibly faked.

Wonder Woman falls into a time warp and meets her double. Flash's alter-ego (Barry Allen) uses super-vibrations to climb a midair rope and accidentally vibrates into another Earth (where he meets Jay Garrick, the Golden Age Flash). Eventually the entire Crime Syndicate of doubled characters gets imprisoned in a void between multiverses.

Then there's the revelation of: Earth-Two.

Two-Face first appears in *Detective Comics* #66 with the name Harvey Kent (later "Harvey Dent"—to rhyme laterally with Clark Kent). Before our own *vis-à-vis*, we were best friends with the enemy, making us more ruthless now. Two-Face's story is rewritten to match his arch enemy's tragic past, because what Motherland or Fatherland doesn't cause beastly offspring?

To make a decision, Two-Face flips a two-headed coin.

(A coin with two heads always wins—
unless one face is scratched out by an X, as he is rumored to do.)

Earth-One and Earth-Two show what's possible when a massive nuclear weapon splits a country. Germany, Korea, Vietnam, Ireland: walls are needed for projection, M.A.D. spies are dropped behind the lines, to mine the split, captured and turned back wearing superhero cloaks. That's infrastructure, a *lit de fortune*. What anyone (not in the room) says is controlled before it reaches the intended audience. All propaganda can be seen as censorship and information in equal measure; *le mal du pays*. Spies need both sides of the conversation or there's no connecting the bug house lines of paper ants. *Honni soit qui mal y pense.*

I have a funny foreign accent; I am a bad guy.

You have a funny foreign accent; you are the bad guy.

Are we both thinking what I'm thinking? Are you running me or am I running you?

> *"I know exactly why Guy Burgess went to Moscow. It wasn't enough to be a ~~queer~~ Santa and a ~~drunk~~ Santa. He had to revolt still more to break away from it all. That's just what I've done by becoming an ~~American~~ Santa citizen."* (W.H. Auden)

In *Two-Face Strikes Twice*, Two-Face must fight Paul Janus, who is two-timing his wife. Sometimes, Two-Face has twins. In another, Two-Face becomes healed. Then Two-Face is taken over by impostors. Some are not really two-faced but use makeup. It would be entertaining if we didn't feel ourselves implicated.

> *"We were venturing, like spies, into an enemy stronghold. 'They,' our adversaries, would employ other tactics down there; they would be sly, polite, reassuring; they would invite us to tea. We should have to be on our guard. [. . .] the whole establishment seemed to offer an enormous tacit bribe. We fortified ourselves against it as best we could, in the privacy of our rooms; swearing never to betray each other, never to forget the existence of 'the two sides' and their eternal, necessary state of war."* (Christopher Isherwood, traveling with Edward Upward to Cambridge to interview for admission)

Then there's Earth-Prime, where everything seems the same as Earth, until a character interferes with Soviet and American missiles, and nuclear war ensues.

> Meanwhile, in space, double planets have "tug of war" sizes, and mass ratios of close to 1, so many doubled bodies don't quite qualify . . .

We wonder why we've been so lucky.
In each pair, there's a primary—and
a more deadened, yet alternate planet.

Pluto and Charon, both icy, dance in the rebound
of a cosmic collision.
Like Earth, Pluto has a resplendent atmosphere
and colorful surface.
Charon and our Moon do not. Together for billions of
years, we couldn't be more different. Considered almost
invisible, Charon and the Moon start to reveal their
own personalities, their own designs on the plot as they
hold the primary planets in place.

We reminisce about situations where superheroes bounce back and
forth into their cover characters, *la tête à l'envers*, between nations
that are enemies. Just before the feature, an unlucky break!

Your face, then my face, toward the aisle of the theater as someone runs up:

"HALLO!" (screamed like it's been ages) "IT'S
BEEN AGES!"

is that an old friend?
an invasion across newly formed identity
(the friend did us a favor once . . . we might be
compromised)

(Pulse, even respiration, normal pupils undilated)
friends blow cover more quickly than any "non-offi-
cial cover operative"
(everything is a border test)
blank space (in a book) masses behind defense
(erase us through identification)
(Every drunk young man or woman is a trap)
every offer to buy a drink after the movie
every encounter a lie (detector)
yet we attempt to soften the subject (calm the mon-
strous frenemy) to get a cover, you must first lose
your identity.

COVER UP, UP, UP!

Movie monster Lon Chaney, first proletariat of
disguise. His deaf parents afforded him a childhood
pantomime (with results refracted in the amplitude
and abundance of his expressions). A mission fits

the covering; a mission is fiction. They called Lon "boy of a thousand faces," and in the silence of horror films he projected the terrible deformity that keeps attention from the person undercover. Even under the most hostile interrogation, the fiction remains fact.

On radar, spies are trained to see familiar shapes from the top—as warships, planes, antenna shadows . . .

Lon Chaney created and built his faces himself, and his secrets have never been revealed (taping his ears, prosthetic attachments, wigs, putty, greasepaint, false teeth, costume . . .). In the Paris Opera, his is the original misunderstood monster. His son will play another, Larry Talbot slash The Wolfman, whose cover-up was documented frame-by-frame, from the fingers pinned and plumped, to the yak hair on his face.

The war between sides comes home, they say, but the bugs in homes needn't worry. There are over 10,000 specimens from basement to roof, over 100 species of arthropod in a single house. Flies and beetles, ants and wasps, stink bugs, book lice, moths, millipedes, silverfish, cockroaches, fungus gnats, cobweb spiders, scuttle flies, dust mites—all harmlessly among us unnoticed, doing our undercover work. Carpet beetles eat spilled food, nail clippings, hair—while dust mites eat dead skin. Book lice eat our books, head lice our hair, the perfect cover.

After the great war, we screen ourselves:

The Spy Who Came In from the Cold
Torn Curtain
The Man Between

A listening post? Is that how a friend behaves? The aftershock, the lasting feeling that enemies mutually benefit— creates a stable (cold) situation of distrust, without open fire, only the assurance of total mutual annihilation. Flip. Flip. Now there aren't many things we both see the same way, looking out in identical opposite ways. You'd think our species had split in two.

A leaf blows across the windshield at a drive-in, and everyone places their trash by a door, their books in the car window, spine out. These are the signals. Nothing isn't right there for normal people to see if they look, but who looks the right way? It takes a prop department to set the city with dead drops: a decade of long-finned cars (the chase element, the movie weaponized with foldout machine guns and camera eye-wear). Nationalism seduces the audience to the sight of movie monsters two hundred feet high, with fries and a soda, with your sweetheart everywhere around you, a last resort, a moon one-faced toward Earth. Under the Outer Space Treaty, our shared moon is open for peaceful business while the dark side hides.

Sherlock Holmes: "Nothing is more deceiving than an obvious fact."

"IT'S BEEN AN AGE!" a second dangle.
You try to duck, pulling me down.
Is the reversed friend enough in this Age of Information?

Someone says:
"Well, the Stone Age didn't end because they ran out of stones."

(something new puts it out of business)

But can you define a friend without the term?
You turn violently, and I'm facing the "stranger."
"So glad to see you again."

Do balance our alterity, at least until the risk of
more violence passes.

"The perfect friendship destroys itself."

Or a friend = a split soul across us, two from one, a
translation.

"A trace of strangeness easily enters even the most intimate
relationships . . . what is common to two is never common
to them alone . . . No matter how little these possibilities
become real and how often we forget them, here and there,
nevertheless, they thrust themselves between us like shadows, like a mist which escapes every word noted, but which
must coagulate into a solid bodily form before it can be
called jealousy." (Georg Simmel, "The Stranger")

A handler must before all else know the inner mind
of the handler on the other side, though they may never meet.
After all, they both see out of one pair of double eyes. Why
can't a double agent become a triple one? Are there that many
ways to lie?

"Does your best friend insist on kissing you whenever she sees
you? Does she constantly brush up against you, even in the
most intimate places, seemingly by accident? Does she love
to brush your hair, watch you undress, and buy you presents?
Then beware. She may be trying to seduce you!" ("Is Your
Friend a ~~Lesbian~~ Santa?" *Dare*, 1957)

If the coin is grabbed by an enemy midtoss, what will we
do? *Se mettre en quatre.* I've said it a thousand times if I've said
it once: "A private eye is not a spy."

(There's no debugging a home, and a spy has no friends.)

And a spy is not a traitor. The spy is an enemy soldier behind our lines, while the traitor betrays familiars to strangers.

And a heretic is not a conspirator.

It doesn't matter if he looks perfectly normal. Beware of strange men who strike up conversations in bars, trains, and other public places.

Beware of doubles who lurk just behind and pretend to understand your orbit, your version of things.

Flip.

In mutually assured death: treat others as you would they treat you. Just as a spy doesn't exist without an enemy, he can't succeed without diminishing that enemy to a final point, a symmetry versus an asymmetrical bend of social space: a ~~physicist~~ Santa versus a thief.

June 21, 1927, *New York Times*, "Einstein, Robbed of Everything in His Home, 'Applies' Relativity to Trap Thieving Maid":

Yes, relativity applies to honesty!
Einstein returned to his home and found it bare of all his things.
"*Cherchez la femme!*" said the Berlin police, quoting a French aphorism, and Einstein tipped them off to his servant, whose boyfriend was found lounging on Einstein's Louis Seize sofa. The servant herself was found in her Rhineland village dressed in Mrs. Einstein's furs and finery.
Einstein maintains it was relativity that exposed dishonesty.

To be a ~~monster~~ Santa: run in and out of shadows, standing in them. Beat. Beat. A costume can be anything. But before you become a monster, tell someone. You'll need a handler. Don't go it alone, don't "borrow" material without permission or put talc or shoe polish on your face or use glue or rubber cement directly on your skin. Clean up what you spill. Warts require tissue and liquid-skin adhesive. Blood needs food dye, paint, and Karo syrup. Gauze makes prosthetic face-parts, and old false hair gives sick effect. Sounds include ticking clock, bending a metal sheet, tinkling bells, scratching nails against cardboard. Of course, to change from Jekyll to Hyde before their eyes, you use red and green makeup in alternating red and green light. Lighting tricks allow ghosts to appear and disappear as well. With just a balloon and an extra-large shirt, you can make a floating head!

We've been tailing the ~~scientists~~ Santas because they're Earth's latest superheroes. Destroyers. The ~~scientists~~ Santas have very long tails. ~~Scientists~~ Santas are rational actors. They are non-state actors. They only believe what they can see.

December 23, 1954, *New York Times*, "Einstein Baffled by Santa Problem: He Cannot Decide at Anti-War Film Whether Christmas Spirit Is Real":

"Define terms," he insists.

"*Scientist Chuckles at Hitler on Screen Here and Wants to Know About Journalism*"

After viewing an anti-war film, *Dealers in Death*, about munitions makers, Dr. Albert Einstein, waiting for his car in the lobby, is asked by a persistent journalist: "Is there a Santa Claus? Do you believe in the Christmas Spirit? The Spirit of Santa Claus?"

"Spirit?" Einstein echoed. "First you must define your terms."

Asked again, the Professor refused to be rushed. "I will think about it till tomorrow."

The statement that "Hitler's Reich can have no durance" was made the night before by Dr. Einstein at the Brooklyn Jewish Center where a ceremony was held for the inauguration of an American Library to contain books burned and banned in Nazi Germany. Pointing out that every community based on hatred is "predestined to decay," he continued that "these wounds seared on the soul of the German folk will block any road toward a sound community basis, even after the people will have freed themselves externally." Greetings were also read from André Gide in Paris, and Bertram Russell in London.

It's possible, with much violence, to hold a peaceful line which can't be crossed back. Propaganda (one's own lies) creates a double image, a regular-person Santa game; "I can't remember where I put the mark." Whether you kick the bucket or *lâche la rampe*, believing your own propaganda raises susceptibility to the ghosts and noises of a haunted bedtime.

"There may possibly be still another partial explanation for the warped mentalities of the spies; namely, an almost diseased yearning to remold the world after the image of their own work in physical science. The study of subatomic particles, the behavior of neutrons, the nature of fission— an attack upon these problems, however difficult, might seem orderly and rationally satisfying compared with the intangible complexities of moral and political issues. To an immature mind such as Fuchs' ~~Communism~~ Santas may have had special appeal because of a seeming resemblance between the regulated order it would impose upon society and regularities in his own laboratory research. In any event, it is evident that a lack of moral standards, combined with an overweening and childlike arrogance—all induced by exposure to ~~Communist~~ Santas recruiting techniques during early manhood—characterizes the atomic spy." (CONGRESS'S JOINT COMMITTEE ON ATOMIC ENERGY—SOVIET ATOMIC ESPIONAGE, APRIL 1951)

Essentially, what you hear is a plot point breaking into faces that break into faces as fast as the earth spins through plot points past-now and future-now:

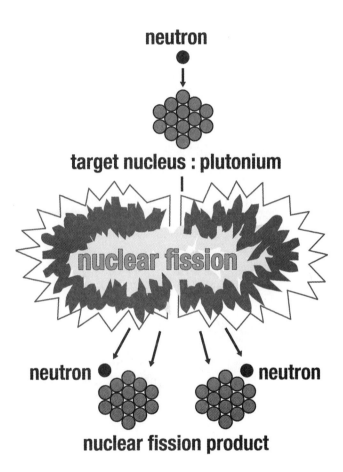

SUNSPOTS

In a split second, lowly resident agents such as we are (never more than satellites to the great goings-on) get launched from impending retirement (between the next wars occupying our foreign and familiar country), shot forward to case out the universe, or just around the room, listening in, making an about-face, making another, covering it all up, denying what happened, seeking objects from outside our solar system...In other words, is there a more important holdover than the left-overs of who is a friend and who is an enemy?

It's a new old age.

Disruption still spans distraction.

The object is longer than it is wide, longer than previous objects were, and unique, as though it were designed to distract us from everything we know. "It's moving so fast the sun can't capture it into its orbit."

Distraction distorts. Distortion impedes. Impediments paralyze. Paralysis withers.

The old days aren't just new again. "It very much came without warning," the scientists insist, "But there is no need to panic." They call this new object: '*Oumuamua* . . . Hawaiian for 'a messenger from afar who gets there first.' And yet, it will leave the solar system and never come back.

The Sultans of 17th century Constantinople welcomed the embassies of all nations, without ever sending out an ambassador of their own.
Why should they?
As with Rome, the spies and interpreters lined up to be loyal always to the other, with a party attitude, and the diplomatic corps was born.
Bilinguals ruled the day, hear in one ear and speak in another tongue, the earliest *dragoman* was a renegade or Levantine, and those non-European sweetwater Franks could sell translation and secret services to all. Dragoman to one embassy was usually brother or cousin to the dragoman of the next. Never to be trusted, loyalties turned inward, or to the highest bidder. Other complaints included changing royal titles to subservient ones to please the Sultan—so that the Holy Roman Emperor was merely "King of Vienna." Code Names translated the other way,

the full title is restored so intention is masked. No matter
which way one is heading, the service of foreign power
is always the mysterious ethics of translation through
interpreters.

Our current pre-occupation comes closer to this state of
affairs, every instant can be simulcast, an entrance/exit
threshold between opposite nations bound in chemical
signals. We are animals. We scent our kind. Notionally foreign
equals nationally native, illegally profitable, are we simply
genetic puppets, carried on the fists of others, dangling into
hemispheres, or just simply pheromone spheres, of influence?
                              (who **cleaves** to, who **cleaves**)

Pulled from retirement at a moment's notice, are we not one
planet, but two? Four? Are there not a lot of other earths and
near-earth objects now, just waiting for intelligent life? Who
we are in the future is not continuous with today unless we
maintain our connection. What will we recollect when our
faces make a head-on collision? Satellites orbit and transmit, a
degraded role. Which of us will play the newly formed moon,
and which the earth meteor-struck? The meteor never did. The
news goes both ways. Has history become more obsolete? We're
long in the tooth on that.

                    (Two that **cleave** to fuse a Head—
we stare from a window between words, behind wordlessness.)

A rich man drives the plot. Rich men replace information with
ownership (fate) and rocketships and it's all sold as the most
natural thing, this last supper at the Chinese restaurant, in a
Paris owned by others, launching our menus into space.

We've been hiding in a rented room, near the runway, subject
to occupancy and alternating currents where there's no air

conditioning (again) and sweat catches at our neck, glistening
at the base of the throat, at the gutter of folded messages, in
the base of the bearded and beardless. The temperature rises in
some corners, and freezes in others. We tussle about where to
sit. We settle on the bed.

We have been handled, we have been brought to heel. Rich
men have knocked. We have opened the door. By force or chill
we shake ourselves side to side, channeling (recalling) a bridge,
our central channel combines our double-faced adulthood—
was it so bad?
          neural or astral, our spine spans the bed, to fuse, to
centrifuge—to cross ourselves a few more times—as we spin
in the lonely apartment in an occupied foreign country of our
native land, waiting to be redeployed.

          Two mouths make lonely sounds as the chill
                    rises up our throat:

          "Is 'lonely' the past? Is 'lonely' the group?
       Is 'lonely' the feeling of never being faced head on?"

Old agents normally simply slip into silence, or are
brought in cold, so easily it's said of friends and enemies
that the heat makes things rise, that we are nouns to
possess or discard. Even in outer space, there's not really
absolute zero. We've stripped the apartment to almost
nothing, no Louis XVI sofa, no fancy car, for example,
and yet space is instantly full when we think about it, like
all our trash looking back.

Is that you, on the bare mattress turned away, not wearing fur,
posing questions as we wake? Sweating away the afternoon,
after too much sleep, your face unknown to me as always; a
distant suspicion never verified.

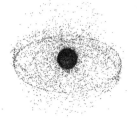

"Did I speak," I feel you thinking.
Our bodies are sore, our minds are soft.
"Is that you?"
Despite our handicap, or due to it,
we are still fit for certain ends.

Plato, The Symposium: *"According to Greek mythology,
humans were originally created with four arms, four legs,
and a head with two faces. Fearing their power, Zeus split
them into two separate parts, condemning them to spend
their lives in search of their other halves."*

How, one might wonder, have we never been truly united,
with our shared organs and self-same physiology? Haven't
we always stood together? Our feet on the right side of the
line, even with our different views? Can't there be two right
sides? Is the face such a thing of division?

Aren't we just one body? In disease or in health?

We'll find out, perhaps, as our launch will finally cut us
loose—now without the old stuff of spy-craft—but rather—
privately sponsored surveillance. The new wars profess no
need of human intel, and certainly not the days of kit-
tens and donkeys and shadows cast by airplanes. Even gates
are virtual, and only virtual citizens pass through, open for

numerical decoding. We're asking, basically, to return dust to
the stars, to sprinkle intel into the widest net imaginable, in
case a reader exists on another planet to make sense of it.

The day before launch, leaving the apartment at high noon,
windows fogged, sleepy from too much lying around,
we orient our last dead drop on the moving target. Park
benches are comets, duct tape is nuclear fuel. It's all in a
day's work, but lest we get too cocky and old-fashioned,
we learn how to play mere cut-outs in the chain, snippets
of basic DNA ready to mutate or split. The wrong choices
made so long ago leave no way to win in less than one kind
of infinity. It's a draw. That's what we tell ourselves, anyway.
We're launched pawns of infinite chess—played as decoys
and sweetened honey traps, never to be brought in. . . or
made queen. The debris is magnificent—it circles around
and never quite touches us, burning on re-entry.

We take comfort: the launch day is optimal, and we have
sort of prepared.

> We piece together how traitors dusted us
> and stole what hides in sight, twisting
> the few Janus-words we trusted—
> Seemingly random figures and flights of history
> congealed and sweating in the hot air—
> while the sun, we will learn, is not really yellow
> (it's all atmosphere and tricks)
> and friendless we become every friend
> despite the endgame of *faux amis*
> escaping to dream machines beyond the heliosphere
> another legend
> at the threshold of our radiant mutation,
> at the bridge between what we wanted and what we got:
> the gate comically/tragically stuck open.

Separating will be painless, they promise,
you've always sensed it.
Is that true? Can a doorway be split in two? Can peace be split?
Suddenly you seem about five hundred million,
maybe 2 billion miles away.
"It's an honor to be asked, a tremendous responsibility," we
mumble into the speaker from our distinct mouths.
Your turn. I turn.
"This isn't just AIR America or Alliance Base"—Turn.
"This is a much bigger and more critical assignment."
Turn back.

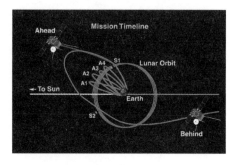

Good thing the planet was never worth a second look.
Wasn't it?
Good thing we were never attached to any small farm, or
village, or meal. Weren't we just customers between wars in
the Chinese restaurant in Paris?
Flip a coin for who trails the earth and who goes ahead.

> (They call us: Solar TErrestrial RElations
> Observatory-*Ahead* (**Stereo-A**); **B** is for *Behind*)

> Funny, that nostalgia, of a simple stroll across the bridge.
> Funny, how it didn't really matter what we called it.

You laugh once, and I fall silent. There are no further
euphemisms for this dilemma—just big worries. Once we
leave the planet, we give up the right to a horizon, quaint
sunsets, hummable melodies, hellos and goodbyes, little
sayings used poorly.

> Step right, step left, turn an elliptical phase, spin

(sometimes you see something, sometimes I do, but we're
both spinning on the target—
spinning to catch sight of ourselves)—

Together, triangulating with our angles, we can approach
a portrait. This is how, separated but still dual-facing,
we'll capture the first complete image of the
back of the sun.

Remember when I told you I'm glad it's worked out this
way, because my safe mode on the sun's backside allowed
some valuable **me-time**, free from the need to transmit
messages that would be hard to interpret anyway?

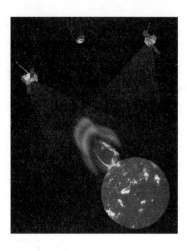

Remember?

Well, now that my three months are up, I've got enough.

It's your turn behind the star,
            the curtains billow, arms sweating as we scissor-leap
and crack these solar eruptions—
the inventors said to give a three-day warning yell if we see hostile solar wind, flares, sun-storms coming to disrupt—
                        Outside of comic book covers, we can now
                              confirm from this distance—
                                    there is no Earth Two.

(We get famous all of a sudden.)

The broadcast studio, cup of water the size of the
Mediterranean, journalist asking:
                        "So why did you become double-agents?"

(Trick question! We rotate, steady into our staring. Spin to
yours; we are on auto pilot out here in orbit.)

"Was it the money, or some inflated need of excitement?
Was it some ideal like patriotism or religion?
Was it ideology pure and fine? Or maybe, think back,
was there a grudge or a loss of affection? Were there real
wrongs or even fictional ones? Or was it just the
nature of feeling so alone. . ."

"Did this all make you feel important and give you thrills?"

Our wrongness is making us famous even more. Our
mumbled non-responses due to global language processing
failure. There are not enough too-many languages.

We can't recall if I blackmailed you, or if you did me. Were
we wannabe Mathilde Carrés? Did one of us know just that
little extra something that provided coercion? Did you just
slip in, or did I wake one day on a skull's protruding face?
How did we get into this hot mess?

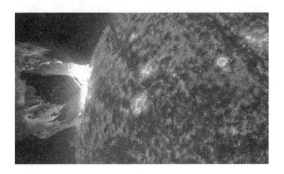

Prompted by the microphone, we go into a rambling
description of planetary chemistry (those classes we slept
through in high school are now on instant replay) the
powerful disrupting (deceiving) signal (hand-shakes and
head nods—left right, up down are just old ideas)—how we

were taught: translator, traitor—the once-a-century storms
that seemed always at our threshold—

> "Yes, high school was hard on everyone.
> We just naturally stuck together."

The backside of the sun is always a gigantic double-entendre.

Donne-moi la parole—and then I'll know it's still you back there.

Our once-human mind wanders, the once-human streets
bustle, you make a concerned expression, I'm caught in a
greeting. Just like old times. Should we rotate to show ourselves fully? Half and half, eyes askew? What would the rich
men make of us then? How can we be sure we're seeing the
same enemies, or that we're from the same team? The saint is
a singleton, a single-face, so we think, and so has he no dark
side, no back side, no opposing view?

The Persian empire translated its laws into 127 languages.

Bilingual inscriptions on the Rosetta Stone show rulers making themselves understood. Pliny said the Caucasians spoke so many languages the Romans needed 130 interpreters to deal with their kings and princes.

More parties. More fame. More pressers.

Coming apart is a coming out!

> "You've both been elite-trained,
> your R2I as strong as they come."
> "You never gave in to an enemy, even if it's yourself?"
> "What are you thinking when you're the one double-speaking?"
> "Do you still call it: 'effective talking'?"

Contradictions, *faux amis.*
Reader, the garden of trust must be tended.
O my friend, there is no friend.

The once-human streets offer more quaint reconnaissance: we gather solar rays full of positrons and anti-protons, and file a quick report on thinly folded atoms, their creases a world between, a brush with death's pocket, when a thunderstorm makes a burst of anti-matter—

Rushing back to the apartment, the stars fall and we fail to brush our anti-hair, or close an anti-door. We plan a little anti-walk across an anti-bridge. . . Loss of information is vexing, if optimism in a predictable system fails. Is that our job anyway: to stand for optimism, and that a past emerges from the future?

Lonely it is to be outside the door and realize the same inside.

Punch is a security code. A puppet murderer. One Janus Patulcius, the other Janus Clusius, one open one shut, one hot season ending as the next begins. . . Armies stampede for the next battle. The Janus gates mostly stay open during the annihilation of cities and civilizations. One foot is the process of a particle's collision with its anti-foot, the step an anti-step. Minus one plus one, yet everything is preserved in zero sum. Path and anti-path ever so briefly at rest at the gate's center.

Here on the edge of the mattress, things get messy the more you try to guess me, the less I can be known, our demeanors forever hidden no matter how quickly we spin. Falling to the floor, dizzy, we try the trick a thousandth time. To spin to see each other's face, even for a fraction of a second—a virtual pair until we collapse. You offer two up quarks and one down, while I have two anti-ups and one anti-down—fuel for rocket ships come of this stuff. And duct tape.

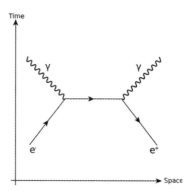

"You're not my friend," you spit out, reading me wrongly or perhaps on the right side, as I spin us around.

Will I be left at the border, or you?

Guilty? Innocent? Nobody cares that I drown in an anti-sea,

or you breathe anti-air. Nobody wants to read on anti-paper about what's going on at the edge of our anti-nation. If we are **rent**, if we find ourselves in a tide of governmental forces, won't we mutually surrender to gravity, leading to a common anti-gravity escape?

Donne-moi la parole; we're covered in plausible deniability.

Dance with me: I can shuttle the view of my horizon into your retina, I can stimulate my memories into your biography. Sharing your body, we can both have ears on the scene, I can fetch and carry the buckets of time up the muddiest slope and not spill a drop, even as I reverse myself into your amphora. Remotely, from your other side, my car is steered, my hologram sworn on, my fetish fulfilled. This, my sworn doppelganger, is how we know we have been done for, corrupted in our common fate as enemies-in-waiting. Every drop of salvo I deliver with such gravity, so carefully into your countenance, to wet your tongue and dissolve your meal, behold, to be beheld, binds us in a push-pull of security and indifference.

At yet another press conference, later in the week, the reporters flashbulbing, the curb hidden in pants:

> "Everyone knows that the morning star
> and the evening star refer to the same star."

The next launch attempt is called off. Who is our man, our woman in the situation? Who has ears on the planet?

Some kind of blowback from being blown. We hope not.

Were we burnt so fast, so far?

We were supposed to man that mission and signal the

most radical drop-point, some meteor working both sides,
before all the information disrupted by the magnetic rip,
the sun turned finally; a macro-evil chagrin, when the hate
we've toyed around with looks childish by comparison—
forcing us to reveal ourselves as humans first and foremost,
whose solar bubble is our last protection, our final scene
and scare.

BLUE NOTES

To put ourselves outside everything we've done, we become
twin Voyagers in interstellar space, making our way to exit the
solar system in the merest 30,000 years.

per aspera ad astra

Despite the gathering of trillions of truckloads of wasted
information, long lines at the pumping station to send it out
beyond memory, there's one thing we forget:
              it's just a thin magnetic field between us and our
open secret.

Spies will persist even in a global blackout, the sun will
persist to light the blackout in its turn.

Reader, if at any point along the way, we had wanted to
scramble you and win advantage, we could have become
unpredictable. We could have swerved, gotten high, slow,
disrupted your decision-making, disoriented your reading
of what you think you know. We could have really gotten
inside your head and screwed you up. If we had made
decisions at a faster rate, accelerated past your reactions,
like this, we could have, at any point along the way, left you
behind, flailing. This is how agility can trump raw strength.

Or contrariwise: a stream of constant action could have given us the advantage over your reactions. Our strategic distractions might have blockaded you from the start.

But together we face, spinning, our common threat: the sun's magnetic reconnection, each of us bending the other's field, oppositely directed, a low arcade of loops, painful as they are, releasing new energy from our pent-up magnetism, helixes violently expanding energized particles and cosmic rays toward earth, a shock wave to bend the planet's magnetosphere, dangerous to living beings at high altitudes, and capable of wiping out all signal and transmission.

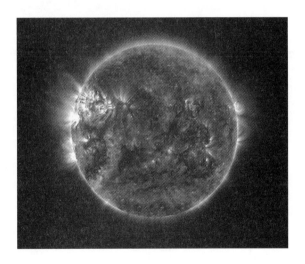

—with the coming storms on the sun surface, the sky's taste is bitter, metallic—

and leaving hurriedly, the apartment littered with take-out Chinese dinners, we laugh, raising each an eyebrow. We can't help moving along in time. We don't need to stop along the cabled highways to conduct our neural networks—the tongue attaches to bone, the nerves spiking the *pons*. We'll sweep satellites and ocean cables. Tastes we cannot share, our tongues whip out to grab the molecules as we fly through our last bites of dumpling. We will win by the oldest chemistry there is, even as the planet boils, or the magnetism reverses, or all the vertebrates curl up. We are metallic, and we taste it in our blood. We are electric, on our fragile grid. We remember side-saddling the couch to take turns watching that tv show we liked.

The television show was moon-based, some old humans in naked night raids that eyes could play tricks, the whispers of trees and owls. It's not that forest night any longer in this city skeleton, and the moon is a lost light, reflected on humans overdone, though we appreciate the nostalgia, and watch another few episodes.

The sun: "A system whose reach is unlimited but whose safe-guards are not."

> "I whisper this," or you do,
> because you realized, and then I did,
> that we may be "the only double-agents
> who quit the earth."

We can't both be first, last, but we can feel that way together. Is intercepted communication all there is once we enter the stellar wind? The sun sends its communications unequivocally.

Now as then, Voyagers 1 and 2, we split Janus-wise, and dance the edge of our heliosphere, survive solar flares, and pass the final gate into interstellar space, as galactic particles from other neighborhoods buffet our now-separate cases. We cut across space but we still twin. We find there is no evidence of shifting in the magnetic field beyond our bubble. Out here, for real, we barely know ourselves and fear we are hardly real in the minds back home. Either way, we will run out of electromagnetic communication. The memory of what it was to have faces will still be here, though, locked in the vinyl disks:

Though most communication follows little scripts, endless tiny variations on a limited number of situations, we plan to meet up safely with whomever awaits us, a small series of lines and a few clues make the translations run, and if each part plays, then we are safely friendly, aren't we?

What passes for intelligence for the future inhabitants of the system? Can they traduct or translate our royal letters?

In Ancient Greek the disk says: *"Greetings to you, whoever you are. We come in friendship to those who are friends."*

Or, in Arabic: *"Greetings to our friends in the stars. May time bring us together."*

The Indonesian takes a reverse approach: *"Goodnight, ladies and gentlemen. Goodbye and see you next time."*

When we go extinct, the hour's worth of recordings will contain the memory of the mouths that formed the words.

> I thought you said, "infidelity is a bad translation."
> But your back is to me for the first time.

You back away, you face my back, so are we finally dancing?

Once again, we ask why the information is so important and to whom?

> "Fools gold contains the tiniest specks of the real thing."

For all the varieties of split-truths, the winks within the blinks, the secrets in the confessions—for all the synonyms and antonyms, the *faux-amis*, does silence always say the same thing?

In Nepali, the disk says: *"Wishing you a peaceful future,*
  from the earthlings."
In Serbian: *"We wish you all the best, from our planet."*
In Rajasthani: *"Hello to Everyone. We are happy here,*
  and you be happy there."

There is a three-day delay from sun flare to an assault on our planet's armor, passing through the threshold of our thin surfaces, to cleave us bloodied down the middle.

In those three days, hemispheres prepare for electric shutdown.

We put an hour worth of brain waves, translated through computer, onto one of those disks. Is it the one you have? Along with pictures of the sun, the solar system, and other important clues.

"This is the biggest hand-off of our careers,"
our handlers must have thought.
Those two will never know what hit them.

We're carrying off all the top secret stuff, to make the cosmic drop:

DNA structure, cell division, chemical definitions, a diagram of
conception, family photos, demonstrations of licking, eating,
and drinking, continental drift diagram, fallen leaves, X-ray
of a hand, diagram of vertebrate evolution, the Great Wall of
China, rush hour traffic in India, dolphins, eagles, a page of
Newton's System of the World, sunset with birds, Jane Goodall
and her chimps.

—my god! Those aliens will have it all!
And we even sent them the decoder!

EXPLANATION OF RECORDING COVER DIAGRAM

Oh, friend, there is no friend.

How can you translate the spinning with our eyes closed
until we are fall-down dizzy? Can we be so far apart and still
be so attached?

Latin: *Salvete quicumque estis; bonam erga vos voluntatem habemus, et pacem per astra ferimus.*

A home is not like any other thing and it's not fungible so easily across the threshold or out the gate where the armies go.

We, *Celestus Janitor*—doorkeeper of the heavenly court— built it where it was not before, where other living things were. It is lived in and cared for, or let to ruin, it can regenerate, or deemed so, and it can be left alone to sleep. It is behind and ahead, the palimsest of houses on maps read by expert spies, or decoded in weird gestures, or hiding between other landmarks and newspapers casting shadows. This is the Janus gate we heard tell. New things can grow in and through an old house until its remains are dark matter and microbial, holding us in place, even as we are here and not.

Michel de Montaigne: *"We are, I know not how, doubled in ourselves, so that what we believe we disbelieve, and cannot rid ourselves of what we condemn."*

From space we turn and spin away and turn again toward the whole old place, including our last apartment. It wasn't so great, in retrospect, in what we understand in space-time as hind- and fore- sight. In fact, we always seemed confused by the past and what was being asked of us.

Speaking in this way, we record another language greeting, and source another source. We become another set of eyes and ears, we double-down on the intelligence. We are at the bridge waiting for the next agent, turned like an equal sign whose reversals can be reversed across change. Despite the persistent symmetry at the heart of the problem, legends are read in the mirror, and words appear as ripples or pebbles, depending on the question.

Reader, there might be an incredible piece of intelligence to bring with us wherever we're going.

Image Credits

1. Two Headed Turtle. AP Photo/Matt Rourke. 26 September, 2007.

2. Anonymous. Laureate head of Janus/Jupiter in quadriga driven by Victory; ROMA raised on outlined tablet. Circa 225–212 BC. Courtesy of Classical Numastic Group, Inc. <https://www.cngcoins.com/>.

3. M. Furius L.F. Philus. 120 BC. AR Denarius (19mm, 3.94 g, 12h). Rome mint. M FOVRI LF. Courtesy of Classical Numastic Group, Inc. <https://www.cngcoins.com/>.

4 (frowning)–5 (smiling). Rare Vintage Chinese Four Faces of Buddha Silver Figurine. Photo of Happy Face and Sad Face. Used with permission of iCollector.com.

6. Santa Claus Listening. Photo courtesy of Matti Mattila. <https://flic.kr/p/dDK9Hd>.

7. Henri Philippe Petain und Adolf Hitler. 24 October 1940. Photographer Heinrich Hoffman. Bundesarchiv. Bild 183-H25217 / CC-BY-SA 3.0.

8. Pach Brothers. Richard Mansfield as Dr. Jekyll and Mr. Hyde. [Between 1885 and 1900] Photograph. Retrieved from the Library of Congress, <https://www.loc.gov/item/96511898/>.

9. Two Headed Calf. Photo courtesy of William Warby. <https://flic.kr/p/X4CvVS>.

10. Death Of Ganelon. From a manuscript of the Grandes Chroniques de France, Paris, BNF, Fr. 2813, fol. 124r.

11. Portrait of Benedict Arnold. From Barbeé-Marbois, F. (1831). Complot d'Arnold et de Henry Clinton contre les États-Unis d'Amérique et le général Washington. Paris: Delaunay.

12. Two Headed Cat. AP Photo/Steven Senne. 29 September 2011.

13. Heracles and Cerberus. Side A (red-figure) from an Attic bilingual amphora, 530–520 BC. From Italy. Department of Greek, Etruscan and Roman Antiquities, Sully, first floor, room 43, case 21, Louvre Museum. Photographer: Bibi Saint-Pol.

14. The Arrest of Christ in the Garden of Gethsemene (The Betrayal): detail of frieze on right inner angle of central portal, West facade of St.-Gilles-du-Gard, ca. 1140s-1180. Used with permission of Allan T. Kohl.

15. Kidwelly Castle, a jagged view. Photo courtesy of Athena's Pix. <https://flic.kr/p/5ADazG>.

16. The Pont Neuf Wrapped. 1985. Christo and Jeanne-Claude. Used with permission.

17. Sipapu Bridge. Photo by Jacob W. Frank. National Park Service.

18. Tacoma Narrows Bridge collapse. Prelinger Archives, 7 November 1940. <https://structurae.net/photos/26-tacoma-narrows-bridge-collapse>.

19. Panorama of Prague, Czech Republic. Photo by john mcsporran. <https://flic.kr/p/rnqmq4>.

20. Double living root bridge in East Khasi. Photo by Arshiya Urveeja Bose. <https://flic.kr/p/9LpNDz>.

21. View of Caesar's Bridge over the Rhine. John Soane. Sir John Soane Museum London. <http://collections.soane.org/THES67825>. Used with permission.

22. Trail & Bridge. Photo courtesy of Tristan Schmurr. <https://flic.kr/p/6R9KVh>.

23. Foto. Bamboe brug bij Malang, Java. Woodbury & Page. Circa 1870. Collectie Stichting Nationaal Museum van Wereldculturen . <http://collectie.wereldculturen.nl/Default.aspx?ccid=9434&lang=>.

24. Donghai Bridge. Courtesey of Zhang 2008. <https://en.wikipedia.org/wiki/Donghai_Bridge#/media/File:Donghai_Bridge.jpg>.

25. Skyway Bridge. <http://wp.wiki-wiki.ru/wp/index.php/%D0%A4%D0%B0%D0%B9%D0%BB:Skyway_Bridge_4.jpg>.

26. A side view of the Remagen Bridge in March 1945 before it collapsed into the Rhine. Claude Musgrove, U.S Army photographer, 164th Engineer Combat Battalion. <http://www.sharonherald.com/image_3b92bf13-328f-5f92-b4b9-cc89d5e7b377.html>.

27. Marcel Duchamp, «Door: 11, Rue Larrey (Porte: 11, Rue Larrey),» 1927. © Association Marcel Duchamp / ADAGP, Paris / Artists Rights Society (ARS), New York 2017.

28. Marcel Duchamp, «La Bagarre d'Austerlitz,» 1921. © Association Marcel Duchamp / ADAGP, Paris / Artists Rights Society (ARS), New York 2017.

29. Marcel Duchamp, "Fresh Widow," New York 1920. © Association Marcel Duchamp / ADAGP, Paris / Artists Rights Society (ARS), New York 2017.

30. Photo courtesy of Nico Michiels. - Whitfield J: Everything You Always Wanted to Know about Sexes. PLoS Biol 2/6/2004: e183. doi:10.1371/journal.pbio.0020183.g001.

31. Photograph of Marcel Duchamp. Victor Obsatz/Moeller Fine Art, New York 2018. Used with permission.

32. Marcel Duchamp, "Objet dard," 1951. © Association Marcel Duchamp / ADAGP, Paris / Artists Rights Society (ARS), New York 2017.

33. Man Ray, "Tonsure (rear view), 1921, Marcel Duchamp." © Man Ray Trust / Artists Rights Society (ARS), NY / ADAGP, Paris 2017.

34. Man Ray, "Marcel Duchamp as Rrose Sélavy." © Man Ray Trust / Artists Rights Society (ARS), NY / ADAGP, Paris 2017.

35. Man Ray, "Mary Reynolds," c. 1925–1935. © Man Ray Trust / Artists Rights Society (ARS), NY / ADAGP, Paris 2017. Image from Mary Reynolds Collection, Ryerson and Burnham Archives, The Art Institute of Chicago.

36. Man Ray, "Mary Reynolds and Marcel Duchamp." © Man Ray Trust / Artists Rights Society (ARS), NY / ADAGP, Paris 2017.

37. Plan du pont Saint-Benezet, profil en long, vers 1680 (AD Vaucluse E DEPOIT AVIGNON Pintat 75-2453). Courtesy of Archives d'Avignon.

38. Double Head of Pope and Devil. Anonymous, 17th century. Museum Catherijneconvent, Utrecht.

39. Avignon confluence, document: Plan de 1618 en huit planches, planche 1 (11Fi136). Photo credit: Maryan Daspet. Courtesy of Archives d'Avignon.

40. Avignon, document: Plan de 1618 en huit planches, planche 2 (11Fi137). Photo credit: Maryan Daspet. Courtesy of Archives d'Avignon.

41. Ezelsbrug or pons asinorum (1763; KU Leuven, Centrale Bibliotheek, ms. 304, fol. 131).

42. Pons Asinorum. *The First Six Books of the Elements of Euclid: In which Coloured Diagrams and Symbols are Used Instead of Letters for the Greater Ease of Learners*, Oliver Byrne, ed., London: William Pickering, 1847.

43. "Devil's Bridge near Ardino, Bulgaria" Courtesy of Vassia Atanassova. (*Spiritia*). 31 July 2006. <https://upload.wikimedia.org/wikipedia/commons/5/57/ Devils-bridge-Ardino1.jpg>

44. Pons Asinorum. Peter Tarteret. <http://www.dbnl.org/ tekst/_tij003191801_01/_tij003191801_01_0013.php>.

45. LROC WAC mosaic of the lunar nearside [NASA/GSFC/ Arizona State University]. December 2010.

46. The Capture of Christ. 13th century. Giovanni Cimabue. Fresco at Church San Francesco, Assisi, Italy.

47. Santa fun runners warming up. Falmouth, Cornwall. Photo credit: Rod Aliday.

48. *The Invisible Man* set photo. James Whale. Universal Studios.

49. Actor Peter Lorre as Franz Becker in the 1931 film *M*.

(Photo by John Springer Collection/CORBIS/Corbis via Getty Images).

50. An ultrarare specimen of conjoined twin harbor porpoises, caught in the North Sea in May. (Courtesy of Erwin Kompanje).

51. Pluto and its moon. Photo credit: NASA.

52. Promotional Studio photograph, Lon Chaney with makeup kit. *The Phantom of the Opera*. Metro-Goldwyn-Mayer.

53. Lon Chaney Jr. in *The Wolf Man* (1941), Universal Studios.

54. "Tree Stump Bug" and
55. "Hairbrush Concealment." Courtesy of the International Spy Museum, Washington, D.C.

56. Far side of the Moon. Photo credit: NASA.

57. Earth and Moon. Jet Propulsion Laboratory, Galileo Project, NASA, 1992. <https://nssdc.gsfc.nasa.gov/image/planetary/earth/gal_earth_moon.jpg>.

58. Nuclear Fission. <http://nagasakipeace.jp/english/record/about.html>.

59. Telling a friend may mean telling the enemy, Poster/lithograph, J. Weiner Ltd., 1942. Victoria and Albert Museum, London 2017. Used with permission.

60. Orbital Debris Model around Earth. Photo credit: NASA.
60 bis. Space Junk. Photo credit: NASA.

61. Trumputin. Photo credit: Dominique Pasqualini.

62. Graphic of "mission timeline" with elliptical phasing orbits.

Johns Hopkins University Applied Physics Laboratory (JHU/APL).

63. Artist rendering of the twin STEREO spacecraft studying the sun. Johns Hopkins University Applied Physics Laboratory (JHU/APL).

64. A coronal mass ejection hurling plasma from the sun. Photo credit: NASA.

65. Vienna, Schönbrunn gardens, statue Janus and Bellona. Photo credit: schurl50. 27 January 2007.

66. A Feynman diagram showing the mutual annihilation of a bound state electron positron pair into 2 photons. Courtsey of Manticorp.

67. The other side of the sun. Photo credit: NASA/STEREO.

68. Voyager Golden record. Image credit: NASA/JPL-Caltech

69. A technical readout on how the Golden Record cover diagram displays information Photo credit: NASA/JPL.

Selected Dalkey Archive Paperbacks

www.dalkeyarchive.com